THE LONELY BUCKAROO

Leslie Scott

CHIVERS
THORNDIKE

This Large Print book is published by BBC Audiobooks Ltd, Bath, England and by Thorndike Press®, Waterville, Maine, USA.

Published in 2005 in the U.K. by arrangement with Golden West Literary Agency.

Published in 2005 in the U.S. by arrangement with Golden West Literary Agency.

U.K. Hardcover   ISBN 1–4056–3170–8 (Chivers Large Print)
U.K. Softcover   ISBN 1–4056–3171–6 (Camden Large Print)
U.S. Softcover   ISBN 0–7862–7029–2 (Nightingale)

The text of this Large Print edition is unabridged.
Other aspects of the book may vary from the original edition.

Set in 16 pt. New Times Roman.

Printed in Great Britain on acid-free paper.

British Library Cataloguing in Publication Data available

Library of Congress Control Number: 2004111180

CHAPTER ONE

Although Cabeza De Vaca was the first European to see it, four hundred years ago, and Count Barnado de Galvez, Viceroy of Mexico, gave it its name, it was Jean Lafitte, notorious Barataria buccaneer and pirate, who raised the curtain and first trod the boards—when he wasn't making somebody else walk the plank—in the opening scene of the drama that was and is Galveston.

Blaine Mason had heard the story of Galveston's inception and the vicissitudes of its early turbulent years from oldtimers who in turn had heard it from their sires and grandsires. He was pondering it as he sat his horse and watched the last of his cattle being ferried across the two miles of water to the island. That herd was the last Mason would ever ship from the Bar Six ranch, for Mason had sold the Bar Six only a week before. The payment was in a moneybelt encircling his lean waist. The money the herd would bring would join it. After that? Mason wasn't sure. One thing was certain, he'd had enough of the coast with its storms and its damp heat. He might return to the Panhandle from whence his father had emigrated a dozen years back when he, Blaine, was only thirteen; or perhaps go to the lower Rio Grande Valley or the northern

1

Big Bend country, both of which he had visited and admired. The death of his father a year before had severed the last tie that held him to south-eastern Texas. Even Arizona wasn't beyond the realm of possibility. He had enough money to get a new start most anywhere he chose. He'd pick a spot where the climate was more to his liking. Meanwhile, a few days in Galveston wouldn't go bad. He'd been looking at a cow's tail for so long that a change of scenery would be welcome. He chuckled as the last tail sailed across to the island. Ferry service for himself and his horse was provided and a little later he stabled the cayuse, attended the weighing in of his cows and received payment. It was long past dark before all the incidentals were taken care of. Mason had something to eat and went to bed in a hotel favoured by cattlemen. After a seventy-mile drive that had taken the better part of a week he was thoroughly tired out. On the morrow he'd hold a last conference with his range boss, Ralph Ames, who was going to work for Jasper Rader, the new owner of the Bar Six. Ames would take his horse back to the spread where Radar had promised to look after it until Mason sent for the critter, a big sorrel named Amber, Mason's pet saddle mount.

Mason slept late. There was no hurry. Ames and his cowboys would carouse most of the night and would be in no condition to talk business before noon. Mason enjoyed the unusual luxury of not having to get up until he was darned good and ready.

After he had dressed he glanced at his reflection in the dresser mirror. He saw a tall man, a little over six feet, broad of shoulder, deep of chest, with tawny hair inclined to curl. Pale grey eyes looked back at him from the mirror, seemingly paler because of the deep bronze of the lean, high-nosed face with its rather wide, humorous mouth and prominent chin and jaw. The man in the mirror wore conventional rangeland garb—soft blue shirt open at the collar with a vividly coloured neckerchief looped about the sinewy throat, clean new Levis, high-heeled half boots of softly tanned leather, and a broad-brimmed 'J.B.,' well worn. A cartridge belt encircled his waist, and from the carefully worked and oiled cut-out holster protruded the plain black butt of a Colt forty-five.

Mason grinned at the man in the mirror with a flash of white, even teeth, cocked the Stetson jauntily over one eye and went in search of some breakfast.

He enjoyed a leisurely meal at a nearby restaurant, smoked a couple of cigarettes over a final cup of coffee and then set out to locate Ames and the boys. He had a very good notion where he would find them, at the Crystal Bar, their favourite hang-out in town.

The Crystal Bar was a big saloon, one of the

biggest and most orderly in Galveston. It did a roaring business, especially at night. Located on Centre Street just off Broadway, it occupied a strategic position. It boasted a long bar, a lunch counter, dance floor, three roulette wheels, a faro bank and numerous gaming tables, and a huge glass chandelier that gave it its name. It was owned and operated by Sam Gulden.

Sam Gulden was a giant of a man with a blocky face, a tight mouth and hard and watchful dark eyes. He was an urbane host but could be plenty salty when necessary. Gulden had other interests besides the Crystal Bar. He owned some real estate and dabbled in local politics. Some said Gulden was power at City Hall. Anyhow, Gulden packed considerable influence in Galveston and was credited with being ruthless in his dealings, although he also enjoyed a reputation for being scrupulously honest.

As he expected, Mason found Ames and the Bar Six punchers lining the bar of the saloon, along with quite a few waddies from other neighbourhood spreads.

'Sort of putting out last night's fire before we head back to the ranch,' Ames explained. 'What did you do last night?'

'I went to bed,' Mason replied. 'Expect I'll mosey about a bit tonight.'

'I envy you,' grinned Ames. 'Just getting the taste of the thing and I have to quit. Oh, well, another payday coming, and another bust. Hate to lose you, Mason, but I reckon we'll make out. Maybe when you get settled you'll send for us.'

'I wouldn't be surprised,' Mason returned. 'If I manage to tie on to a holding in a section I like, I'll be needing hands.'

'You'll get 'm,' Ames declared. 'Understand Jasper Rader isn't a bad man to work for, but we'll be glad to get back with you.'

'Glad you feel that way, Ralph,' Mason replied. 'Yes, the chances are I'll be sending for you.'

Sam Gulden came over to shake hands. 'Understand you're leaving us,' he remarked. 'Be sorry to see you go, but I know how it is with a young feller. Ain't no cure for itchy feet but to go places. Been around a bit myself in my time. Getting old, though, and have to settle down. Have one on the house.' With a smile and a nod, he strode back to the far end of the bar where the till was located. Mason reflected that Gulden never got very far from that till for any length of time. He reflected that somehow Gulden's smile never seemed to reach his eyes, which remained expressionless, slightly opaque. Mason didn't particularly care for the man, just why he couldn't say. He certainly could not complain of Gulden's attitude the few times he had visited the Crystal Bar.

Ames and the cowboys said goodbye and

departed for the ferry and the Bar Six. Mason wandered about the town, looking things over. He ate a late dinner, then prowled some more, having a drink here and there, dancing a few numbers with the dance floor girls in the saloons and generally enjoying himself. He was relaxed and slightly mellow when he finally gravitated to the Crystal Bar about midnight. Gulden greeted him with a wave of his hand and turned back to the till. Mason found a vacant table, sat down and ordered a drink. He rolled a cigarette, lounged comfortably in his chair and watched the crowd, sipping his drink. He felt dreamy and content and, with his second drink, increasingly drowsy. He eyed the glass owlishly, raised it to his lips, emptied the last of its contents. Faugh! He'd had enough; the darned stuff was beginning to taste bitter. He belonged to bed. And that was where he was going to head in just a minute. Right now he didn't feel like moving. So darned sleepy! He nodded, roused with an effort, nodded again. He leaned forward slowly, pillowed his head on his arms. His eyes closed.

Mason vaguely realized that he was walking along a poorly lighted street between two men. Rather, he was lurching and stumbling, his feet, strangely heavy, dragging on the rough sidewalk, a hand on either elbow supporting him.

'What the heck!' he mumbled.

'Take it easy,' one of the men said. 'We're

6

taking you to your room; you passed out.'

Mason turned that over in his foggy mind. Nice of them. Who were they? Didn't matter. They were all right. He shook his head, dislodging some of the cobwebs that swathed his brain, and began to think almost coherently. His mind was clearing just a little, enough to dimly sense that a hand was drawing his gun from its sheath. The cobwebs dissolved a bit and he realized his danger. He jerked free from the hands that gripped his elbows, lashed out with his left fist. His knuckles landed solidly on a man's jaw. There was a gasping curse and the thud of a falling body. Instantly he was the centre of whirling fists and feet. He connected again, his fist boring deep into a midriff and bringing forth an explosive grunt. Then light blazed before his eyes and he pitched forward on his face, all but unconscious. From a great distance he heard a voice demanding, 'Here! Here! What's going on here? What's all this?'

Another voice replied, 'He's blind drunk and was starting to raise Cain. Gulden told us to take him home and put him to bed.'

'Okay,' said the first voice. 'Get him out of here. You blasted cowhands are always making trouble. They ought to bar the city to you. Get going! Get going!'

Mason was hauled to his feet, his knees buckling under him, and hurried along. He struggled feebly. Again there was a blaze of light before his eyes, and a pain shooting through his head, then blackness.

CHAPTER TWO

When Blaine Mason recovered consciousness, he was lying on a narrow bed, clad only in his underwear and his boots. He lay on his back, and as his eyes opened slowly he found himself staring up at a white-washed ceiling where five cracks came together to form a device. The cracks swooped down and stabbed him in the temples. He closed his eyes quickly and kept them closed. Finally he opened them again, cautiously, wondering mistily if the cracks would renew their onslaught. They wavered a little and took on colour, red-bronze like the Texas sumach in the autumn, but remained where they were. He closed his eyes against the little trickles of pain still weaving in and out about his temples, opened them even more cautiously. The cracks remained cracks, dusty greyish streaks against the white of the ceiling. His eyes snapped open and he struggled to a sitting position, retching as a wave of nausea swept over him. He gripped his pounding head in his hands and breathed in choking gasps.

Gradually his mind cleared and he fought down the cloying sickness. His head still throbbed, but the pain was not quite so sharp.

He dropped his hands and took stock of his surroundings.

He was in a small room with a single window. It was furnished with the bed, a cheap dresser and a chair. Across the back of the chair were draped a pair of patched and dirty overalls and an equally dirty shirt with holes in the elbows of the sleeves. His own new Levis, shirt and Stetson were nowhere in sight. He did not need to reach for his waist to know that the plump moneybelt containing more than forty thousand dollars in big bills was gone.

The explanation of what had happened was simple enough. Drugged and robbed! He recalled the slightly bitter taste of the last glass of whisky. Yes, that was it, drugged and robbed! Lucky he hadn't been murdered, too. There was a cut on the side of his head where a gun barrel had landed. A sizeable lump just above it indicated where the second blow had connected.

His mind was whirling again. Abruptly he realized that he was shivering with cold. Getting cautiously to his feet, he struggled into the patched overalls and the ragged shirt. They helped a little. He was fastening the last button when a light tapping sounded on the door. He went rigid, fists clenched.

'Come in,' he called hoarsely and poised, ready to spring.

The door opened very slowly and a man

9

shuffled in, a very old man whose hair was white. His face was a network of wrinkles but his eyes were bright and kindly. He stared at Mason.

'Thought I'd better see how you were making out,' he said in a creaky voice. 'You didn't look so good last night when those two fellers brought you in.'

'Two fellows brought me in?' Mason repeated.

'That's right. They hired the room and lugged you into it; you weren't walking very good. Said they'd put you to bed. I didn't think much of it. I'm always getting fellers who've had a snort too many packed in. Plenty of that here on the waterfront and I don't pay it much mind. They come down after a bit and said you were sleeping.'

'Did you know them?' Mason asked.

'Nope, never saw them before,' replied the oldster. 'Cowboy looking fellers; they were dressed that way. Say! You don't look to be dressed the same as when they brought you in!'

'Reckon I'm not,' Mason answered grimly. 'They only left me my boots. Guess they were too small for the hellion who tied on to the rest of my clothes.'

The old man clucked sympathetically. 'Rolled you, eh? That happens here.' His shrewd old eyes scanned Mason up and down.

'Son,' he said, 'you don't 'pear so good right

now, but you look to be the right sort of a young feller. There's water in the pitcher over there on the dresser. Fill the bowl and dunk your head in it, then stretch out on the bed again. I'm going to the eating house down the street and get you a bucket of hot coffee and something to eat. Don't leave the room— you're in no shape to be on the street. Wait right here till I get back.'

Before Mason could protest, he hobbled out the door and closed it behind him. Mason could hear his feet labouring down the stairs.

The water in the pitcher was cold and fresh. Mason swallowed some of it, for his throat was parched. Then he filled the bowl with the remainder and made shift to wash his face. Feeling a little better, he straightened up and dried his face and hands with a rough but clean towel that hung on a nail by the dresser. Then he sat down on the edge of the bed and tried to think. He was still trying, with scant success, when the old man returned, bearing a steaming bucket and a paper-wrapped parcel.

'Get on the outside of this and you'll feel better,' said the old fellow, thrusting the bucket into his hands.

Mason drank the coffee gratefully. It was almost too hot to swallow and sent warmth and strength surging through his veins. Over the rim of the bucket he eyed his benefactor.

'Where am I?' he asked.

'Water Street, just off Centre,' the other

replied. 'Can you rec'lect anything of what happened to you?'

'I was drinking in the Crystal Bar and I guess I went to sleep,' Mason answered slowly. The old man shot him a shrewd look.

'The Crystal Bar,' he repeated. 'The place that feller Sam Gulden runs. Gulden is a sort of big he-wolf in this town. Knows all the folks at the courthouse and City Hall. And you went to sleep in there, eh?'

'That's right,' Mason said. 'Next I knew I was on the street with a couple of fellows shoving me along. There was a tussle and they knocked me out. That's all I remember till I woke up here.'

'And cleaned your pockets, eh?' nodded the old fellow.

'They certainly did,' Mason replied grimly. 'Cleaned me for every last cent. They—wait a minute, maybe they didn't get everything, at that.'

He placed the bucket on the bed beside him and tugged off his left boot. With eager fingers he felt inside it. Yes, it was still there, the little wad down on the toe. He drew forth two crumpled twenty-dollar bills.

'Sort of a habit of years to pack them there,' he explained to his companion. 'Fellow riding around can never tell when he might need a few extra pesos. They look mighty big right now,' he added with a wry smile. 'Anyhow, I can pay you for the coffee and the sandwiches.'

12

The oldster said cheerfully, 'I don't take pay for lending a mite of a helping hand to a feller who's had a bit of bad luck. Did those sons take much off you?'

'Considerable,' Mason replied briefly. The old man clucked and shook his head.

'Eat your sandwiches and drink the rest of the coffee 'fore you talk any more,' he advised.

As he munched the sandwiches, Mason endeavoured to orient his mind to circumstances as he found them. At one fell stroke he had been reduced from affluence to poverty. He had no doubt as to who was the instigator of the outrage. He recalled one of the devils mentioning Sam Gulden's name to the marshal or police officer who had happened on the fight, with whom Gulden's name would carry weight. Gulden knew, of course, that he had sold his ranch, and he had wormed it out of Ames or one of the hands that he carried the money on him. Gulden had fed him drugged whisky and engineered the robbery. What could he do about it? Denounce Gulden? He wouldn't have a leg to stand on. Gulden would disavow any connection with the affair and make it stick. In Mason's heart a black and vicious hate was growing. Perhaps it was a good thing that the hellions had taken his gun. Right now he was in a mood to shoot Sam Gulden on sight.

But what would that gain him? The hangman's noose or a long prison term were

13

too heavy a price to pay for revenge. There must be some better way to even the score. Mason resolved to find a way. He had an answer ready for the rooming-house keeper's question when it was asked.

'What do you aim to do, son? Go back to your ranch where you work, I suppose.'

'No,' Mason answered. 'I'm going to stay here in Galveston, that is if I can tie on to a job.'

'I can fix that for you, if you don't mind hard work with a rough bunch.'

'I'm used to hard work, and I think I can hold my own with a rough bunch,' Mason replied.

The old man ran his eye over Mason's broad-shouldered frame and nodded. 'Yep, I've a notion you can,' he conceded. 'Son, my name is Klingman, Caleb Klingman.'

Mason supplied his own name and they shook hands. 'Tell you what,' said Klingman, 'I'm going down and get you some more coffee. It's just the thing for a feller in your shape, and I got some salve that will be good for that cut on your head. An old Karankawa Indian, there aren't many of them left, made it up for me and it's prime. Wasn't anything much the Karanks didn't know about salves and poultices and the like.'

'Yes, they were the poison people of the Texas Indians,' Mason observed.

'Uh-huh, they were pizen, all right, plumb

pizen,' said Klingman. 'That's why the whites just about wiped them out; there was no taming them. After a while we'll go see about that job. They need men on the waterfront. It's hard work, but you can make good money on the docks, a heap more'n by following a cow's tail. There's plenty of overtime for them that wants it, and skippers in a hurry to get out of port will pay mighty well for that overtime. I know Jeth Bixby who runs a big gang; he'll be glad to take you on. Okay, see you in a minute.'

'There's one more thing you can do for me, if you don't mind,' Mason said. 'Take one of these twenties and buy me a clean shirt and overalls, and a hat. That will hold me for the time being. And some tobacco and papers,' he added as an afterthought.

'I'll do it,' said Klingman. 'I got a hat that I think will fit you—too big for me, but it's a good one. Some feller left it in one of the rooms—they're always leaving things—and here's tobacco and papers you can use till I get back. When a feller wants a smoke, he wants it. Back in a minute.'

He shuffled out. Mason gratefully rolled a cigarette with the slim fingers of his left hand and smoked with deep satisfaction. Physically, at least, he was feeling a lot better. His head had stopped aching and the food and hot coffee had neutralized the effects of the chlorodyne, or whatever it was the devils put in

15

his drink.

Mentally he was still in a seething turmoil. He would no sooner try to think than the flames of his anger would rise and sweep away all coherent thought. Sam Gulden! His rage came on again like a gust of wind. Only one thing, cold and clear-cut, focused sharply in his disordered mind: his resolve to wreak vengeance on Sam Gulden. How? At the moment he hadn't the slightest notion, but there must be a way; he would find a way. He rammed down his rising wrath with the iron hand of will and dragged fiercely on his cigarette. He mustn't go off half-cocked. By doing so he would play into Gulden's hands. Whatever he hoped to accomplish would take time and patience. Grimly he resolved that patience would be his watchword. He could wait for his hate. Its consummation would be all the more gratifying for having been delayed. He'd get his money back, and he'd crush Sam Gulden if it took the last breath in his body.

Gradually something definite took form. There would be something better than killing Gulden, a torture transcending the physical. Mason believed that he suddenly beheld the key to a most exquisite vengeance on Sam Gulden. Gulden was ambitious, and to destroy the fruits of such a man's ambition is to destroy the man. How? Mason didn't know, but there must be a way. He rolled another cigarette and relaxed on the edge of the bed. With resolve had come an easing of tension and clarity of thought. He was smoking comfortably and his hands no longer balled into anger-trembling fists when old Caleb Klingman re-entered the room, bearing packages, a fresh bucket of hot coffee and a hat.

'Coffee and chuck's on me,' he said as he passed Mason his change.

'Do you always do things like this for folks you find in trouble?' Mason asked.

'Oh, sometimes,' Klingman replied. 'When the feller looks right. You get to judge folks pretty well in this rooming-house business, and I've been in it for better'n twenty years now. Doesn't do you any harm to help folks out now and then. The wheel turns, you know, and a feller who is on the bottom today may be on the top of the heap tomorrow. You never can tell. And if he's the right sort, he won't forget. Try this hat on for size. I believe I figured the shirt and the overalls pretty well, after looking you over.'

The hat was a pretty good fit. It wasn't Mason's forty-dollar 'J.B.,' but it would do. A good fit, also, were the shirt and overalls. Mason donned them before starting in on the second helping of coffee and sandwiches.

'I feel more like a human being again,' he said.

'Yep, clean clothes will do that for a feller,'

Klingman observed sagely. 'Maybe clothes don't make the man, as somebody once said, but they can do a lot for his feelings. When you've finished eating we'll go see Jeth Bixby.'

'I can keep this room?' Mason asked.

'Sure, for as long as you want it,' Klingman replied. 'Renting rooms is my business. I usually have a pretty good crowd here. Sort of rough, but not bad. Most of 'em work on the docks. All set to go?'

The Galveston waterfront was a colourful scene. Grimy tramp steamers, trim passenger vessels, fruit ships, sluggish, wallowing oil carriers came from a hundred ports to crowd the fine harbour.

Mason had always liked the water fronts of Galveston and other Gulf towns. The prospect of working amid this exhilarating orderly confusion was not distasteful.

Jeth Bixby proved to be a middle-aged, pleasant man with keen eyes.

'Sure I can use you,' he said to Mason. 'You look husky. And anybody Caleb Klingman recommends is mighty apt to be all right. Report here at seven tomorrow morning.'

Leaving the docks, Mason and Klingman headed for Water Street. 'I've got to get back to the house,' old Caleb said. 'What do you figure to do, son?'

'I thing I'll walk around a bit,' Mason decided.

'That's a notion,' nodded Klingman. 'The

fresh air will do you good. When you come back we'll eat together at a restaurant I usually patronize. A nice feller runs it. He'll look after you till payday.'

'With your recommendation,' smiled Mason.

'Oh, I bring him a lot of business,' old Caleb deprecated his thoughtfulness.

'I'm getting mighty deep in your debt,' Mason observed.

'Forget it!' said Klingman. 'The time may come when you can give *me* a hand. Never can tell.'

Mason walked aimlessly through the bustling streets, brushing shoulders with the hurrying town people. Everybody appeared cheerful, gay, intent on their own affairs. Mason abruptly realized that there is no loneliness like to that of a crowded city. A wave of depression settled down on him, and a feeling of hopelessness. How the devil could he buck Sam Gulden! Gulden was a man of substance, respected, with friends in high places. How could he, without standing or connections, by himself, prevail against such a man. On the corner of Ball Avenue and Twentieth Street he paused, gazing with unseeing eyes at a stately building across the way; it was the courthouse.

Gradually he sensed that letters were cut in the high granite facade. They took form, became words —*Yo Solo*—*I* Alone! It was the

19

motto of the City of Galveston.

A fitting motto, Mason absently thought. Truly applicable to that handful of adventurers, the scourings of the world, men defeated, men without country, who had given front to savage beasts and savage men and the dumb imponderable forces of nature, and had won.

Right now he was down at the bottom, with no place to look but up. He had lost his heritage, for that was what it was. He had inherited the Bar Six from his father, had not acquired it through his own efforts. Now it was gone. Now it was up to him: a test of strength, a trial by which he could prove himself worthy. Those old fighters whose shadowy presence he could feel had proven themselves. Now they were expecting him to prove himself. He wouldn't let them down. He was darned if he would! Under his breath he repeated the words that were inspiration—'I Alone!' Turning, he walked back to the waterfront, shoulders squared, head held high.

CHAPTER THREE

Work on the docks was hard, all right. Wrestling cotton bales, barrels of sulphur, huge bundles of green hides, crates of machinery was no easy chore. For the first few days, despite his excellent physical condition, Blaine Mason suffered soreness in muscles he never before knew he had. That passed quickly, however, and before long he could hold his own with the best of the dock wallopers.

As Caleb Klingman said, there was good money to be made on the docks. Overtime was always available, and frantic skippers with their sailing schedules liable to be disrupted were glad to pay well for a helping hand. In addition, Mason was a good poker player and the games always going afforded him opportunity to augment his weekly pay envelope.

Although he steadily saved his money, Mason did not deny himself social life. He caroused in moderation with his fellow workers, with whom he soon became a prime favourite.

'High-pockets is all right,' they'd say. 'He's an educated feller and has been around, but he don't put on the airs. He's one of the boys.'

All in all, things were working out well. Mason felt that all he needed was time and patience to realize his ambition. He was confident that sooner or later opportunity to get on top would come his way. The first rung up the ladder was to be gained sooner than he expected.

Jeth Bixby was a good man to work for. The same could not be said for Gus Kearns, his straw boss, who had the actual handling of the workers. Kearns was a hulking individual with thick shoulders and arms knotted with muscle. He was overbearing, vindictive, and had a nasty temper. Most of the longshoremen were afraid of him, for he had the reputation of being the toughest fighter on the waterfront. They usually took his browbeating in sullen silence.

Kearns early singled out Blaine Mason for special attention. For no reason that anybody could figure, he took an instinctive dislike for Mason and reserved his most vicious tongue lashings for him. Mason took his verbal abuse without comment, for he wished to avoid trouble. But one day, about three months after Mason's arrival at the docks, Kearns made the mistake of putting his hands on him. Mason had not quite understood an order the straw boss had given and was turning to ask a question. Kearns grabbed him by the shoulder and gave him a shove, accompanied with a burst of foul language. Mason whirled around and hit him, hard. Kearns described a parabola and hit the ground with a thud. He bounced to his feet with a roar of fury, and the fight was on, the fight that would be talked about on the waterfront for many a long day.

Kearns rushed, his bullet head lowered, and caught a left hook on the jaw that knocked him sideways but did not discourage him. He came right back for more, boring in, huge fists flailing.

Blaine Mason quickly realized that he had real trouble on his hands. He was far quicker than the massive Kearns and could hit him twice to Kearns' one; but Kearns' blows carried twice the weight of his. Very quickly both men were bleeding. Kearns had ceased to swear and fought in grim silence.

There was very little science on either side. It was largely give and take, hit and be hit, a brutal slugging match. Both were breathing hard, but neither was in a mood to give quarter. This was a fight to the finish, with the chance that the loser would end up a badly injured man.

Mason knew this, and he also knew he couldn't take much more of such a merciless pounding. There was a taste of sulphur in his mouth, a ringing in his ears. His heart was racing, his lungs heaving. He rocked Kearns' head with wicked right and left jabs, staggered him with a straight left to the jaw, but took plenty of punishment himself. The crowd of longshoremen leaned forward in tense silence broken only by the gulps in their throats as the blows landed. They were all for Mason, but this ruckus was too deadly for comment.

The end came quickly. Kearns drove Mason back with a smashing blow to the midriff. The former cowhand slipped on a greasy spot on the boards and staggered off balance. In an instant, Gus had beaten him to his knees. With a yell of triumph, Kearns charged in for the kill.

Mason lunged forward, caught Kearns around the thighs and hurled him over his shoulder, helped as much by Kearns' mad rush as by the expert strength of the heave.

To the bystanders' eyes, it was as if Kearns had taken wings and flown. He hurtled through the air, great limbs revolving, hit the dock boards with a crash, groaned and lay still.

Heedless of the cheers of the dockers, Mason, his face bruised and bloody, staggered erect and stumbled to where Kearns lay and knelt beside the fallen man, more than a little anxious, for the fall had been a heavy one. However, Kearns rolled his head from side to side, groaned a curse and struggled to a sitting position. He glared hatred at the man who had whipped him, got to his feet and, supported by two men who had stepped forward at Jeth Bixby's nod, lurched off for the nearest saloon.

Bixby sauntered forward to where Mason stood trying to fasten the remnants of his shirt about his bruised chest.

'A good wring,' he said. 'Just about the best I ever watched. Well, son, looks like you've took a step up. It's the law of the docks, you know, that if a straw boss starts a row with a man and can't finish it, the man who licks him gets his job. Gus won't be back. He'll go clean to the other end of the waterfront and stay there. So it looks like you're elected. It'll mean quite a bit higher pay for you and a lot more opportunities for making more money on the side. Congratulations!'

The dockers whooped and cheered, and slapped Mason on his sore back.

'Come over to the office and wash up and have a drink,' said Bixby. 'You can stand both. I'll put some plaster over those cuts and you'll be okay. You're a good man, Mason, a good man, and I've a notion you're going to make a darn good boss. Come along.'

Jeth Bixby was right when he predicted Mason would make a good boss. Soon the hardy longshoremen were saying:

'The Old Man's okay. When the going is tough, he's right there with you, and if you have trouble and are in the right, he'll stand up for you till the last cow comes home. Yep, he's one of the boys.'

Blaine Mason ceased to be known as Highpockets along the waterfront. He was the 'Old Man!'

The title, Old Man, has nothing to do with age. Nor does it come with promotion. It has to be earned. The dockers never called Gus Kearns the Old Man; but it seemed natural to call Mason that, the highest accolade men who work with their hands can confer on a boss.

Mason also quickly found plenty of chances to make money over and above his pay. The word got around and a skipper who was in need of a helping hand was told:

'Go to Mason. He'll treat you right and he won't take advantage of you because you're up against it. He can get a gang together any hour of the day or night, and they'll shove cargo like you never saw it shoved before. See Mason.'

And ship commanders who would have bitterly resented anybody demanding an undue profit from their hour of need were generous with the man who could always be depended upon to give them a square deal.

Blaine Mason still lived in Caleb Klingman's waterfront rooming-house, and he had no intention of moving, although he could have afforded better quarters. A firm friendship had developed between him and Klingman. He found the old fellow entertaining and interesting. Cale had been around plenty and knew how to tell a story well. And truth lived in his homely philosophy.

It didn't take long for Mason to confide in Klingman the real story of what happened the night he was drugged and robbed and to reiterate his belief that Sam Gulden was responsible. Klingman's eyes grew thoughtful as they rested on his young companion. He had never seen vengeance so indelibly written on a face, and he had never before realized the terrible power of vengeance. Old Cale felt he would not be in Sam Gulden's shoes for all of Sam Gulden's money.

Not that Caleb Klingman was in need of money. As Mason learned, Klingman was very comfortably fixed indeed. His big rooming-house was always filled to capacity with paying tenants and had been for years. No, Caleb Klingman didn't need money.

'Don't know what I'm going to do with all of it, though,' old Cale chuckled. 'Nobody to leave it to. Maybe I'll have it changed into silver dollars and skip 'em across the bay. You can help me and we'll see who can make the biggest splash. We'll have fun!'

The weeks and the months scampered by. Blaine Mason had become so wrapped up in the waterfront that he hardly heeded the passage of time. There was certainly nothing monotonous about work on the docks. Always there was colour, change, new problems to meet and solve. From all the world men came with strange stories, hints of wars in the making, of scientific achievements that would revolutionize life, of new discoveries. Always there was adventure, vicarious and real. Little wonder that his past life began to seem dim and distant indeed. Mason realized that his viewpoints were broadening, certain opinions modifying. Life which had been a narrow channel had suddenly become a vast panorama that steadily widened. Old ideas were discarded. New ones took their place. His great ambition was still to come even with Sam Gulden, but other ambitions were crowding in. What had once been vague possibilities were now logical probabilities. Looked like maybe

Sam Gulden did him a favour. He chuckled at the thought, but his anger against and his hatred of Gulden were in no wise abated. Because of Gulden he had been down and apparently out. What if he had lifted himself by his own bootstraps! No credit was due Sam Gulden.

Once a cowhand, always a cowhand. So says the rangeland; but Mason was beginning to wonder. He had not lost interest in ranching, but that interest had become greatly modified. At times he doubted if he would ever go back to it in a serious way. To replace monotony, even though it were a peaceful and contented monotony, life had become vigorous, even eventful, an uplifting potpourri of dreams and the real. He felt he was sailing new seas, with new worlds to conquer. And still to come was another venture even farther from anything he had ever visioned.

It was Mason's popularity along the waterfront that afforded him the opportunity for his triumph over Sam Gulden. One night old Cale shuffled into his room and deposited his creaky frame in a chair.

'Heard the news?' he asked. 'Your *amigo* Sam Gulden is running for Councilman in the election next month, the seat left vacant by Wainright's death. There's a good man running against him and it'll be a close race, but Gulden has the backing of the political machine and I reckon he'll win out. I figure he aims to be mayor some day and the Council is a stepping-stone.'

'I suppose the hellion will make it,' Mason replied morosely. 'Seems his sort thrives in politics.'

'Maybe,' conceded Klingman, 'but if he got licked in the race for Councilman it would be considerable of a setback for him. Son, don't that give you a notion? You got a good standing with the boys along the waterfront, and there's a lot of 'em.'

Mason stared at him blankly, then abruptly his eyes glowed. 'Cale,' he said slowly, 'I believe it does. Thanks for putting the notion in my head.'

As a result of the 'notion,' in the days that followed, Blaine Mason put in a lot of time going up and down the waterfront, talking with leading men of the various gangs.

As a rule, the dock workers paid scant attention to municipal elections. They ignored the blandishments of politicians and didn't give a darn who won or lost. Generally, hardly any of them took the trouble to vote, although they were citizens of Galveston and were qualified to do so.

At this particular election, however, it was different. They flocked to the polls, to the astonishment of all and sundry, and voted as they had been requested to vote. The result, a stinging defeat for Sam Gulden, with the votes of the hundreds of dock workers responsible.

Blaine Mason smiled grimly and enjoyed his first taste of victory. And he vowed it would not be his last.

It was inevitable that Sam Gulden would learn who was responsible for the setback to his ambitions. His anger was great.

'What's the hellion got against me?' he complained querulously to his head bartender and, known to but few, his silent partner in the business, a lanky saturnine individual known as Long Tommy who had a cast in one eye that almost covered the pupil and which lent an even more sinister aspect to his sardonic features. 'I never did anything to him.'

'At least nothing you figure he knows,' said Long Tommy. 'Beginning to look like he *does* know, eh?'

'You talk too darn much!' spat Gulden.

'If you don't want me to talk, don't start me talking,' Long Tommy said softly. 'Don't start me talking!' His single eye rested hard on the other's face, and Gulden flinched a little. In his secret heart, Gulden was afraid of Long Tommy who was a killer and who also knew too much. Not good for a man to know too much, he reflected. His eyes grew thoughtful, but he only said:

'No sense in us snapping at each other, but I'm afraid Mason will have to be taken care of.' He shot a meaning glance at the bartender.

'Why don't you handle the chore yourself?' asked Long Tommy. 'You set up to be a big skookum he-wolf. Why not brace him man to man and tell him off? He couldn't do more than kill you.'

Gulden snarled like a cornered rat. 'I ain't no quick-draw man and you know it,' he replied. 'I don't need to be. I can hire all of that kind I need.'

'Well, this time the one you hire had better be good,' said Long Tommy. 'I've heard considerable about Blaine Mason. He's poison with a gun. But of course that doesn't protect a man against a shot in the back, say from the dark.'

'What do you mean?' demanded Gulden, changing his attitude to one of fierceness. But he was well aware that whatever tone he took with his partner, he never fooled him.

'It can be managed if the price is right, as you very well know,' observed Long Tommy.

Gulden drew a deep breath. 'The price will be right,' he said, almost in a whisper.

'Let's have a drink,' suggested Long Tommy.

CHAPTER FOUR

The significance of Mason's ability to swing a municipal election was being given serious consideration in other quarters. Owners and shippers abruptly realized that here was a man with whom they would have to reckon. 'See Mason,' began to be pronounced on land as well as on water, which caused Jeth Bixby to chuckle loud and long.

'Son,' he said, 'it looks like you're going places. Know what they're beginning to call you? The Boss of the Waterfront. But don't forget, son,' he added in a more serious vein, 'power is a two-edged sword. Don't forget.'

'I won't,' Mason promised, not looking into the future to see how hard it might be to keep that promise.

On receipt of his second pay envelope, Mason had bought a gun; he had worn one so long that he felt naked without it. He did not carry it on the docks, but he did carry it when he prowled the streets at night, for Galveston was still a good deal of a wild frontier town where violence was liable to erupt at any moment. He had religiously avoided the Crystal Bar.

Although exhilarated by his initial victory over Sam Gulden, he did not over-estimate it. He had hurt Gulden's pride and had given his ambitions a temporary setback, but that was all. Gulden was still solidly foundationed and it would take a much harder jolt to do him real harm. Also, an angle Mason did not overlook, he had irritated and perhaps alarmed the politicians who ran the city. Reprisals of some sort might be in order. Well, he figured he could take care of that.

The fact that he had created something of a stir in civic affairs was demonstrated less than two weeks after election. A suave gentleman dropped in to visit him at Jeth Bixby's office when Bixby was elsewhere. After a few pleasantries and inconsequential conversation, he got down to brass tacks.

'Mason, the boys up at the Hall have their eye on you,' he said. 'You've got them a bit interested and they figure they can use you. Why don't you come into the organization? We can make it worth your while.'

'I go it alone,' Mason replied.

The other nodded and became more direct. 'Just what have you in mind, Mason?' he asked. 'We might throw something your way.'

'I'm not in politics,' Mason replied shortly.

'Well,' the gentleman said dryly, 'you were sure up to your neck in them a couple of weeks back.'

'I had my own reasons for doing what I did,' Mason said.

'We might be able to advance those reasons,' the other observed significantly.

'Perhaps,' Mason conceded, 'but I think I can do better by myself.'

The gentleman left a little later. He was somewhat baffled. The business was puzzling and, he felt, a bit ominous.

'The young devil's got something cooking in the back of his head,' he told his compatriots. 'But he won't talk.'

'He'll talk when he's ready,' predicted an old-timer.

'Yes, but perhaps then we won't particularly like what we have to listen to. In my opinion, he's going to be a hard man to handle.'

'Every man has his price.'

'Yes,' repeated the emissary to whom had been entrusted the chore of sounding out Mason. 'Yes, but sometimes the price comes unpleasantly high. One thing is certain, he's got the longshoremen organized. He could tie up the waterfront tighter than a drum if he took a notion to do so.'

'Think he might be planning to pull a strike?' asked another gentleman, high in office.

The emissary shrugged. 'Could be possible,' he conceded. 'As you know, labour is organizing all over the country and beginning to feel its power. However, I don't think Mason has anything that crude in mind.'

'What *has* he got in mind?' the other demanded in exasperation.

'John,' said the emissary, 'did you ever hear of the Question and Answer Club? One of the rules was that if a member asked a question none of the other members could answer, each member had to donate a dollar to the treasury. But if the member who asked the question couldn't give the answer to his question, he had to donate five dollars to the treasury. Well, one night a member came rushing in. "Boys," he said, "I've got a question. When a groundhog digs a hole, why doesn't he leave any dirt around the top of the hole?" Well, nobody could answer the question, each had a pungle up a dollar. "All right," they said, "you asked the question—what's the answer? Why doesn't the groundhog leave any dirt around the top of the hole?" "Because," said the first member, "it starts at the bottom and digs up." Well, there was silence for a minute or two, then somebody burst out, "But how the heck does it get to the bottom to start digging up?" "That, brother," said the first member, "is *your* question!"'

After the chuckles had subsided, the emissary said, 'And, John, what you just asked is *your* question.'

Mason liked to walk along the Gulf shore, especially on windy nights when the long lines of great black waves, each with its curling edge of foam, were thundering in endless succession from out of the inexhaustible southeast. He liked the taste of the salt spray on his lips, the feel of the night wind in his hair. Sometimes he would walk far out over the uneven blocks of the jetties to stand in dark-shrouded loneliness under the blazing Texas stars. The stupendous majesty of his surroundings would soothe his spirit and bring a strange peace to his soul.

Although Mason did not know it, these nocturnal prowlings of his were noted with interest in certain quarters. Had he known it, he might well have curtailed or abandoned them altogether.

One still night found him far out on the lesser jetty. The Gulf was calm, the surf but a whispering against the lower stones. It was very warm and suddenly he experienced the desire for a swim in the black water which washed the foot of the massive barrier. He undressed, draping his clothes over an upstanding block of stone and setting his hat on the jutting peak of its corner. As he started to work his way down the sloping side of the jetty, he glanced back and chuckled at the resemblance, in the faint starlight, of the heap of clothes to a man sitting with his back resting against the stone.

It was very dark at the foot of the jetty, but the water was cool and invigorating. He did not venture far out from the sloping wall but contented himself with swimming about near the base of the jetty. After a while, feeling greatly refreshed, he started back up the slope, easing himself slowly and cautiously over the blocks, some of which were sharp edged. He had nearly surmounted the crest and was almost within arm's reach of his clothes when the shoreward darkness gushed orange flame from a distance of less than a score of paces. The hat perched on the peak went sailing through the air. Through the bellow of the reports he heard slugs hammer the stone over

36

which his clothes were draped. He flattened out, his heart going like a triphammer, almost paralysed with astonishment. Then he saw two crouching figures stealing forward through the gloom.

Blaine Mason realized that he was on a very hot spot indeed. The would-be killers were coming to make sure of their work. When they discovered they had been shooting at a heap of clothes, they would immediately search for the wearer of the garments, and his shrift would be short when they found him.

What was he to do? Should he try to scramble back down the slope and dive into the water? He couldn't stay there forever, and he could hardly hope to hide amid the rocks, for soon a nearly full moon would rise in the east and make the whole scene as light as day. His only chance was to get hold of his gun and shoot it out with the devils. With the greatest caution he inched forward, trying to keep in the shadow. The pair, apparently reassured by the lack of sound or movement, were coming faster. They were not much more than a score of feet distant. Throwing caution to the winds, he lunged forward desperately. As his hand closed on the butt of the big Colt, a voice shouted, 'Look out! He ain't dead!' They had seen his white body against the dark stone. He jerked the gun from its sheath, rolled on to his side and fired as fast as he could pull the trigger.

37

Answering slugs stormed through the air. One ripped the flesh of his upper arm, throwing him sideways with the shock. Another grazed his cheek. A wailing curse answered his fourth shot. Peering through the smoke fog, he saw that both men were down, one twitching slightly. He lay rigid, the muzzle of his Colt trained on the two bodies. There was but a single unspent cartridge remaining in the cylinder, and if one of the hellions was only slightly wounded or playing 'possum, that cartridge would have to make good.

For long minutes he lay without sound or motion. Without sound or motion also lay the bodies of the killers. The one had ceased twitching, the other had not stirred since he plunged forward on his face.

Mason decided to take a chance. He leaped to his feet, slewing sideways, weaving and ducking, bruising his bare feet on the rough stones.

The bodies did not move. Mason stole toward them, cocked gun jutting out in front. He knelt beside them. Both were dead.

One appeared long and lanky, the other short and squat. In the faint starlight he could make nothing of their features. He concluded he'd better get out of there, fast. There might be more of the devils around. Besides, he was feeling a bit sick from excitement and loss of blood and was in no shape for another battle. First he ejected the spent shells from his gun and replaced them with fresh cartridges. Then he bound a handkerchief around his bullet-slashed arm, which was still bleeding though not so profusely as before. Getting into his clothes was a chore, but he finally accomplished it and set out for the shore, alert and watchful. He made it before the moon rose. Seeing nothing of a suspicious nature, he set out for Bixby's office where bandages, salves and astringents were kept. No night shift was working at the moment, but there would be a watchman at the office.

Reaching the office, he immediately pressed the watchman into service without offering explanations. Soon the injured arm was cleansed, treated and bandaged.

'And I'd rather you didn't say anything about this, Bert,' he told the watchman.

'I won't, sir,' Bert promised, and Mason felt he would be good as his word. He repaired to his room and went to bed. Before he could do any thinking on the attempt at murder, he was asleep.

CHAPTER FIVE

Later that morning, Long Tommy entered the Crystal Bar and motioned Gulden to the back room.

'Well?' said Gulden, when they were seated

at a table with a bottle and glasses between them.

'Well, I told you he was poison with a gun,' said Long Tommy. 'A little while ago they picked up Blount and Carter out on the jetty, plugged full of lead.'

'Hell and blazes!' exclaimed Gulden, his face livid. 'Do you figure they talked before they cashed in?'

'I doubt it,' replied Long Tommy. 'I got a look at them when the sheriff brought them in. They were both drilled dead centre.'

Gulden heaved a sigh of relief. 'That helps,' he muttered.

'Yes,' Long Tommy nodded, 'and some good came out of the business, anyhow.'

'What do you mean?'

'I mean,' said Long Tommy, 'that Blount and Carter are out of the way. Oh, I know we had plenty on those two sidewinders, plenty to hang them, and they knew it. And it was to their interest to stick with us. But just the same, you never can tell about that sort. You think you've got them held in line, but you can't be sure. A little loose talking on their part might have proved embarrassing. Now they're past talking, and nobody knows what happened to Mason the night he passed out. That is, nobody but you and myself. No witnesses, which is all to the good. And even we don't know for sure what happened. We weren't even there. Couldn't even stand witness against each other.'

Gulden glared at him. 'What do you mean by that last?' he demanded.

'Oh, nothing, just talking,' replied Long Tommy. 'Just talking. Of course there's one person who has a pretty good notion of what happened and who was back of it, or so I think.'

'Who?' gulped Gulden.

'Mason,' said Long Tommy. 'Otherwise why should he be on the prod against you like he is?'

Gulden swore.

Long Tommy suddenly chuckled. 'Everybody's trying to guess what happened to Blount and Carter,' he added. 'Some figure maybe the two skunks had a falling out and drilled each other, although, according to what I heard, the way the bodies were lying didn't make it look that way. Yep, everybody, even the sheriff, is guessing. And it looks like Mason isn't doing any talking, either.'

'Let 'em guess,' growled Gulden.

'Uh-huh, but the question is, how much did Mason guess? If he figures he guessed right, he may come looking for you.'

'He hasn't anything on me,' muttered Gulden, his blocky face working.

'That's right,' conceded Long Tommy, 'but if he's convinced enough in his own mind, he may decide to take things in his own hands. Maybe he figures if he's in solid enough with the Hall he could get away with it.'

'What the devil do you mean, in solid enough with the Hall?' said Gulden.

'I don't know for sure,' answered Long Tommy, 'but I do know that Chauncy Weed went down to the docks and had a talk with him. Weed, as you know, is a sort of trouble shooter for the crowd at the Hall. They send him around to swing folks into line. Wouldn't be surprised if he took a proposition of some sort to Mason.'

'What would the Hall want with Mason?' Gulden demanded.

'You should know without asking,' said Long Tommy. 'There are a good deal more than a thousand men working on the docks, and they have friends in other waterfront establishments. Such a block of votes has to be given consideration and the Hall knows it. Especially when it appears they'll vote whatever way Mason wants them to. There are other elections coming up, you know, and some of the races will be close.'

Gulden drummed on the table top with his thick fingers, his brows querulous.

'Something's got to be done,' he said. 'Something's got to be done.'

'Agreed,' replied Long Tommy, 'but what? I don't think any more "shooting in the back from the dark" should be tried.' Gulden winced.

'It'll have to be something subtle, something

unexpected,' Long Tommy continued. 'And,' he added impressively, 'something that'll look like an accident if it's possible to work it that way.'

Gulden's face was beaded with sweat. His mouth worked nervously.

'I never went in for killings before,' he muttered.

There was a derisive light in Long Tommy's one good eye mingled with something very like contempt.

'But you never had a killer on your trail before, did you?' he asked.

Gulden passed his hand across his twitching face. 'No,' he mumbled, 'I never did.'

'Well, you've got one on your trail now, or I'm a lot mistaken,' said Long Tommy. He stifled a grin at Gulden's reaction. 'So you'd better sort of get yourself prepared to meet him, sooner or later,' he added.

'I haven't carried a gun since I set up in business here,' muttered Gulden.

'Well, I think you'd better start packing one,' advised Long Tommy. 'Then maybe you'll sort of have things evened up if a showdown comes.'

Gulden scowled. His fingers nervously drummed the table top. He seemed to make up his mind, for his hands stopped working.

'I'll do it,' he said. 'I've got to go over to the Hall. I'll buy one on my way back. 'Bout time for you to go to work. I'll be seeing you.'

Long Tommy poured another drink. His derisive gaze followed Gulden's broad back through the door.

'That'll give Mason the excuse he needs for shooting you,' he apostrophized the departed saloon-keeper. 'I've a notion you won't have any more sense than to try and pull on Mason if he walks in here and scares you. Well, that'll be all to the good. I'll all set to take over.'

Meanwhile, Sam Gulden was communing with himself in a similar manner.

'That one-eyed devil knows too much. I've got to get rid of him. Maybe I can pit him and Mason against each other and get rid of both of them. That's a notion.'

The passage of time was called to Mason's mind by an unexpected visitor. Ralph Ames strode into the office one afternoon.

'You darned old wind spider!' whooped the Bar Six range boss. 'So here you are! What the devil you doing here, anyhow? When we never heard from you, we got to wondering where the devil you had gotten yourself to. So today I started asking folks if anybody knew where you went. Finally a bartender at the Silver Rail told me you were down here on the docks. What are you doing here? And why are you here?'

Mason told him, in detail. Ames swore a blistering oath. 'I'm going up to the Crystal Bar and gut-shoot that son and leave him to die sweatin'!' he vowed.

'No, you're not!' Mason replied. 'You'll just

get yourself in trouble I'll have to try and pull you out of. You leave Sam Gulden to me.'

'But what about your money?' demanded Ames. 'That was one hell of a lot of dinero to lose.'

'Well,' smiled Mason, 'the way things are going here, I wouldn't be surprised if I have it all made back before so terribly long. Lots of opportunities for making money down here, and I've always got my eyes open for the big one I figure will come along sooner or later. Don't worry about me, Ralph, I'm doing all right here, and I like it.'

Ames didn't look convinced, but he promised not to start a row with Gulden.

'All right, if you want it that way,' he said. 'I won't go near the joint or I might forget my promise. And I'll make it my business to see that no other cowhand goes in there, either, from now on. I pack a mite of influence with the boys and they'll listen to me. I won't tell 'em why, though. If I did, like as not a bunch of them would get ossified some night and go there and take that place apart and hang Gulden to a rafter. But I'll keep 'em all out and hit that tight-wad where it'll hurt him most, in his pocketbook, the lousy no-good cross between a hydrophobia skunk and a horned toad!'

Ames' chance remark gave Mason fresh food for thought. Ames had the right idea—hit him in the pocketbook. Gulden worshipped

45

money and was ready to chance murder to get it. That he had proved. This was an angle not to be overlooked. Many of the waterfront workers, on the docks and in other establishments, drank in the Crystal Bar. If the word was passed to them, they would go elsewhere and Gulden's business would suffer.

*   *   *

It didn't look much like opportunity, a big but rather rickety old showboat that tied up at the docks. But that showboat was to have a profound bearing on not only Blaine Mason's future but that of the city of Galveston as well.

'I know a feller who works on her,' a loquacious docker told Mason. 'He says she's got good engines and her hull is all right, but she could stand a hammer and nails and some paint on her upper structure. He says she put on a darn good show but has had a lot of trouble. Seems bad luck sort of dogs her. Lost her rudder in a collision with a tug. A blow smashed up her deckhouse. Her star performer, a girl, got sick and quit. He says they got another one to take the place of the one who got sick, but they don't know how well she'll go over with the customers. What with one thing or another, he's scared the feller who owns and runs her will say to heck with the whole business. He hopes not, for he's got a pretty good job in the engineroom. Says

46

the feller pays all right, when he can, and isn't bad to work for. Old feller who knows the show business and that's about all. He figures somebody with git-up-and-git could make her pay.'

Mason listened rather absently, nodding from time to time, for he had other matters in his mind. In fact, when the docker went off to another chore, he forgot all about the matter. It was recalled by old Caleb Klingman later in the evening.

'What say, son?' said Klingman. 'Let's go down and see the show. First time a showboat's been here for quite a while. I worked on one once for a while, on the Mississippi. Sort of liked it.'

Mason hadn't anything particular to do that evening, so he agreed.

'And suppose we go a bit early,' suggested Klingman. 'That way we'll get good seats, and besides I'd sort of like to look things over and see if they've changed much since I was on a boat.'

Arriving at the docks, they found the showboat decorated with strings of coloured lights. A band was playing, and playing quite well, Mason thought. Upon reaching the deck, he gazed about with interest at the novel scene. Klingman, who was thoroughly at home on a boat, began looking things over and asking questions.

'She's a pretty good old tub, but she's sure

had a streak of hard luck,' said a deckhand he engaged in conversation. 'Seems everything's gone wrong during the past couple of months. Mr. Gavens is about ready to jump in the Gulf. That's him over there by the wheelhouse.

'Hey, Mr. Gavens,' he called, 'here's a gent who used to be in the show business on the Mississippi.'

Gavens, a grizzle-haired, sprightly looking man, clean shaven except for a bristling grey moustache, turned around and regarded his visitors. He wore a long black coat, a ruffled shirt and a black string tie. He nodded and came forward.

'So,' he said to Klingman, as he shook hands with both, 'you had sense enough to get out of it, eh? I'm sure about ready to pull up stakes. One headache after another.'

'You should do all right here,' said Klingman. 'All the boys on the docks will be showing up for the show. Wherever Mr. Mason here goes, they follow. See a bunch of them headed this way right now.'

'Well, I can sure use a break,' replied Gavens. 'I've had about all the bad ones I can take.'

'Does the show go over?' asked Klingman.

'Sure,' the other replied. 'We've got a good troupe. Just signed up a little girl who's a top dancer, has a good voice and plenty of looks, and the others aren't at all bad. Most of 'em old troupers who've been around and know how to put on a variety show. Hope you'll like it.'

'I've a notion we will,' said Klingman. 'Well, Blaine, guess we'd better be ambling in and get us some good seats.'

'Come along,' invited Gavens. 'I'll put you in the best, down close to the stage and in the middle.'

The auditorium was a large one and well appointed. It was clean and, so far as Mason and Klingman could see, the scenery and other adjuncts were freshly painted and in order.

'I had things freshened up a bit before I set out on this cruise,' Gavens explained. 'All except the outside, which could stand a bit of going over. Money was running short, though, and that'll have to wait a bit. We've got a good show, though. Change of programme every night for a week, with more skits and acts in the making. If the luck will just break our way for a while—' An expressive shrug completed the sentence. With a nod, he hurried off to take care of his duties.

' 'Pears to be a pretty nice old jigger,' observed Klingman. 'Superstitious, though, like most show folks. He's beginning to believe there's a jinx on his boat; I know the signs. Let something else go wrong and he'll figure he's at the end of his twine and will need to go in for something new. That's the way with his sort. When things don't go right, they feel they've got to turn to something new.'

'May not be so loco at that,' said Mason. 'Sometimes a change from one thing to another is good for a person.'

'I've a notion you've sort of proved that,' chuckled Klingman. 'Say, the boys are sure piling in. Word must have got around that you're here.'

'I'd say, rather, they want to see the show,' smiled Mason.

Klingman was right about the dockers 'piling in.' Already nearly all the seats were filled, and late arrivals were still appearing.

Shortly afterwards the show started. It was a good performance, Mason thought. It was a combination minstrel show and variety acts, all of them better than mediocre. Old Gavens might be superstitious, but he was undoubtedly a first rate showman. The dockers applauded vigorously and appeared to be thoroughly enjoying themselves.

'Looks like the feller is going to get his break,' said Klingman. 'He'll have this place packed every night he's here.'

The curtain went down on a comedy skit that had the audience rocking with laughter. Printed programmes had been handed around, and glancing at his, Mason saw they were to the final act. The programme simply stated, 'SHARON.'

The orchestra began playing soft music. The curtain rose slowly on an empty stage. Then Blaine Mason sat bolt upright in his chair.

A girl had drifted from the wings like a flower swaying in the dawn wind. She wasn't very big, but her figure was beautifully proportioned. She had short curly dark hair, big, darkly violet eyes, a pert little nose, and sweetly turned red lips. There was colour in her creamy tanned cheeks.

'Say,' exclaimed old Caleb, 'she's a looker!' Mason didn't argue the point.

The longshoremen appeared to think so, too, for they broke into a thunder of applause, calloused palms beating together like a roll of drums. The girl smiled, waved gaily to them, and began to sing Stephen Foster's 'Beautiful Dreamer' in a sweet and pure contralto voice.

And then it happened!

Through the double doors that opened on to a ramp leading to the upper deck gushed a cloud of black smoke. Sucked forward by the draught from the open skylights, it billowed into the room.

For an instant there was stunned silence. Then somebody howled 'Fire!' and the stampede was on.

CHAPTER SIX

Panic is a strange thing. These rough and hardy men, who in their hazardous occupation faced death every day without a qualm, were

51

suddenly filled with overpowering fear. Yells and screams arose, chairs were smashed to kindling wood. There was a concerted rush towards the stage to escape the swirling smoke. Instantly the little dancer was engulfed.

Blaine Mason reached the stage in a single bound. Hurling frenzied men right and left, he ploughed his way to where the girl was in danger of being crushed to death. He flung his left arm around her, hugging her close, protecting her with his own body, while with his right hand he jerked his gun and fired three evenly spaced shots into the ceiling.

The explosions drew all eyes toward him. His voice rang out, the voice these men were accustomed to obey.

'Stop it!' he roared. 'What's the matter with you? Are you scared of a little smoke? Quit acting like fools and get out there and douse that fire, wherever it is. Move! I'll shoot the next man who comes this way! Move, I tell you!'

They moved. Order took the place of chaos. They swung about and headed for the door through which the smoke still poured.

'Don't all try to get out at once!' Mason bellowed. 'Take your time!'

The longshoremen obeyed, crowding through on to the ramp but in orderly fashion and without panic, ducking their heads to the smoke. Almost immediately on the deck above sounded prodigious hammerings and poundings and sloshings; the smoke quickly abated. A few moments later a man thrust his head through the door.

'She's out, boss!' he shouted. 'Wasn't anything but a tar barrel caught fire.'

'All right,' Mason called. 'Come on back in here and sit down. The show's going on.'

'Ain't nothing to set on!' somebody shouted. 'Chairs all busted.'

'Then come in and stand up,' Mason told them. Laughter followed the order. Somebody whooped, 'Hurrah for the Old Man!' The cheers were given with a will.

Mason turned to the trembling girl. 'All right, ma'am,' he said, 'you can finish your dance.'

Finish it she did, like the real little trouper she was, and the applause was even more thunderous than before. She had to come back three times before the tumult subsided.

The longshoremen streamed out, laughing and chattering, Mason and Klingman bringing up the rear. Outside they met old Gavens. He was the maddest man Blaine had ever seen.

'This settles it!' he squawled, his moustache bristling in his scarlet face. 'I'm through, done, finished! I quit! I'll sell the whole shebang to the first jigger who makes me an offer. If I can't sell it, I'll give it away! The darn thing's jinxed!'

Blaine Mason suddenly had an inspiration. 'Mr. Gavens,' he said, 'how much will you take for the outfit—the boat, troupe, good will, everything?'

Gavens subsided. His eyes grew shrewd. He studied Mason a moment, then named a price.

Mason smiled. 'I think about half that would be right for a jinxed boat,' he said. 'Especially as I would consider hiring you, at adequate compensation, to run the show. You run the show and I'll take over the headaches.'

Gavens winced at the word 'jinxed,' but he grinned. 'It's a bargain,' he said.

'Just a minute,' Mason said. He turned to Klingman. 'What do you say, Cale?' he asked. 'I can rake up half the price. Will you come in for the other half?'

'Why not?' chuckled old Cale. 'It had oughta be more fun than skippin' silver dollars across the bay.'

Mason turned back to the showman. 'Okay, Mr. Gavens, it's a deal,' he said. 'Tomorrow we'll see a lawyer and have the necessary papers drawn up and discuss your salary.'

'Fine!' applauded Gavens. 'And now come along and meet the slaves you just bought.'

Mason met the troupers and liked them. Last was the little dancer.

'This is Sharon,' said Gavens. 'Guess you sort of met her before.'

'Guess I did,' Mason smiled, 'but it's nice to meet her again in less hectic circumstances.'

'And it was very, very nice to meet you as I did the first time, Mr. Mason,' she said, answering his smile with a flash of white teeth. 'I was beginning to realize just how a sardine in a can must feel.'

As Mason and Klingman crossed to Water Street a little while later, old Cale turned to look back at the showboat.

'I ain't superstitious like that old fool Gavens,' he said, 'but it might be a good notion to change her name. I've heard that will sometimes knock a jinx.'

Mason suppressed a grin. 'Maybe you're right,' he agreed gravely. 'What shall we call her?'

'You suggest something,' said Klingman.

Mason pondered a moment. 'Well,' he said at length, 'we tied on to her here at Galveston, and Galveston's an island. How about The Island Queen?'

'Fine!' exclaimed Klingman. 'We'll have it painted on right away.'

Old Caleb Klingman was a bundle of energy when he was interested in something. Work on the showboat started the very next morning. In a surprisingly short time, with woodwork repaired and glistening with fresh paint, the old boat proudly proclaimed:

THE ISLAND QUEEN
Mason and Klingman, Owners

Dud Gavens, the former owner, with a pocketful of money and free from care, worked wholeheartedly at getting the rejuvenated troupe into the best possible shape for the opening performance which was scheduled for two weeks after the night of the fire.

Although optimistic as to the outcome of his latest venture, Blaine Mason did not give up his job on the docks. He was no longer just a straw boss, but Jeth Bixby's right hand man, and Bixby was the biggest employer of labour on the waterfront. Mason's influence on the waterfront was steadily widening. Other gang masters with problems began coming to him for solutions. The same applied to various ship commanders who had learned that Mason could relieve their difficulties. More and more Blaine Mason was becoming what he was called—the Boss of the Waterfront.

In addition, Mason was able to put his influence to practical use in the interests of his fellow workers. He got them better wages and better working conditions. For employers who were inclined to grumble, he had a ready answer.

'Contented workers give better service,' he told them. 'They take an interest in their jobs and want to hang on to them. I'll make a bargain with you: if after one month you aren't satisfied you've made a paying investment, we'll go back to the old scale.'

He never had to go back to the old scale.

CHAPTER SEVEN

Old Caleb Klingman rubbed his hands together complacently as he watched the crowd streaming up the Island Queen's gangplank, laughing and chattering. There were not only dock workers in that crowd. Numbers of town folk had come to see the show. Very quickly there was only standing room in the big auditorium, and it wasn't long before even that was taken and disappointed late arrivals had to be turned away.

'Another show tomorrow night, folks,' Dud Gavens told them. 'And every other night we feature a change of programme. We'll be looking for you. Come early, and bring your friends.'

Klingman chuckled and turned to Mason. 'She's going to pay off, and pay off big,' he said. 'Looks like everybody in Galveston aims to see the show.'

'And I've a notion it will be the same at Corpus Christi, Port Isabel, Brownsville and other places,' replied Mason. 'We can even send her up the river to Rio Grande City and Laredo.'

'You're darn right we can,' agreed Klingman. 'Son, you sure hit it off right. Fact is, you've just about hit it off right with everything you've set your hand to during the past year.'

'Yes,' Mason said soberly, 'and sometimes it bothers me a bit. Things have come too darn easy for me.'

'You worked hard and fought hard for everything you've got,' Klingman contradicted him. 'Didn't come easy.'

'I still figure it was too easy,' repeated Mason. 'Reminds me of an old saying, 'Such success offends the gods.' I'm afraid they may have a rod in pickle for me. I can't help but think how easily my ranch, the Bar Six, came to me. I didn't work for it. My poor old dad built it up to what it was and when he passed on it fell in my lap. And then it fell out just as easily,' he concluded grimly.

During the two weeks, Mason had learned a good deal about Sharon, the little dancer. She didn't have a husband, and she didn't have a flock of kids, and Sharon was her real name— Sharon Grant. She was alone in the world, her mother having died nearly a year back, her father a couple of years earlier. That made them a pair of orphans, Mason reflected; he barely remembered his own mother.

Few men are fools at all points of the compass, and Sam Gulden was far from being that. In fact, he was not even as much of a fool as Long Tommy thought him. Gulden knew very well he would have no chance with Blaine Mason in a gun fight, and he had not the slightest intention of getting involved in such a

58

venture. If Mason challenged him, he would decline the combat, even if he were hooted out of town as a consequence. Better to be hooted than to be drilled dead centre by a forty-five slug.

But how to get even with Mason! Gulden consumed half a bottle of whisky, smoked several cigars while concentrating on the problem. He conned over Mason's various activities, seeking some angle that might be vulnerable. He contemplated the whisky bottle, poured himself another drink, rolled the cigar from one corner of his mouth to the other, his brows drawing together. He downed the drink, blew out a cloud of smoke.

Suddenly a thought flashed into his brain and sparkled there. He poured yet another drink, downed it at a gulp. A grin of malicious satisfaction stretched his lips. Darned if he didn't believe he had it! He left the saloon by the back door and headed for the Hall.

His cronies at the Hall received Gulden's suggestion dubiously, considering possible reprisals. Suave, urbane Chauncey Weed was outspoken against it.

'I don't favour tangling with Mason,' he said. 'He's resourceful, and he's a fighter.'

'He can't fight City Hall,' said Honest John.

'No?' Weed replied dryly. 'That's been said before, here and elsewhere. But every now and then there rises up a gent who will and does fight City Hall, in various places, and sometimes City Hall has been known to pack a licking. It could happen here.'

However, most of the gentlemen present were beholden to Sam Gulden for favours done and favours expected. They agreed to go along with Gulden's scheme, albeit reluctantly.

Blaine Mason wasn't present when the representative of the Galveston fire department boarded the Island Queen. Dud Gavens received the unwelcome visitor. Two hours later, Gavens burst into Jeth Bixby's office where Mason was busy with some book work. His face was red, his moustache fairly bristling with anger.

'Look at this!' he bawled, waving an official looking document under Mason's nose. 'That mealy-mouth condemned the Queen! Says she's a fire hazard and not safe to entertain the crowds we're getting. Here's a list of the things he says have to be done if we want to keep operating in Galveston, the repairs we'll have to make, and the alterations. A list long as my arm! To do all this would cost more than to build a new boat! Take it to court, Mason! Take it to court!'

Mason scanned the list before answering. He raised his eyes to the showman's face.

'No use to take it to court, Dud,' he said. 'We wouldn't get anywhere. The Hall controls the courts.'

'Well, if we can't do anything about it, we're out of business so far as this town's concerned,' declared Gavens. 'That is, unless you care to spend all that money.'

'If we did what they ask, they'd just dig up something else,' Mason said. 'This is going to require a little thinking out. They closed down the performance tonight, of course?'

'Of course,' said Gavens. Mason nodded.

'I'll drop over to see you tonight, after I've figured what to do,' he said.

'I can't see as there's anything we can do, except up anchor and head for Corpus Christi or someplace,' Gavens replied gloomily.

'Maybe not,' Mason said. 'Galveston is our best money maker, and I don't propose to give up so long as I can figure some way to fight back. I'll see you later.'

Mason could always think better in the open air, so he took a walk along the Gulf shore, watching the waves roll in from the southeast, listening to their majestic music as they broke on the shingle beach. He felt that he had plenty to think about. He could see the hand of Sam Gulden in the affair. Gulden had persuaded the Hall to make the move that would just about put Mason out of business in Galveston. That is, if he was able to get away with it. And at the moment it looked like he could get away with it. The cost of the repairs and alterations demanded was prohibitive. Of course the Island Queen could still show at Corpus Christi and other ports, but Galveston was the big money maker and Mason did not propose to renounce without a fight. There must be some way to circumvent the scheme, and it was up to him to find that way. He was darned if he was going to take a defeat at the hands of Sam Gulden!

Still puzzling over the problem, he walked out on to one of the jetties and stood gazing at the scarlet and gold blaze of the sunset. Galveston Island dwindled away into the west, with beyond that bit of land where very likely Gabeza de Vaca made his first landing, now called San Luis Island.

Mason had once visited San Luis Island and the old seaport town of Velasco just across the Brazos from Freeport. Velasco had served as a port of entry and a Mexican customhouse, and for a time was one of the leading seaports of Texas. At Velasco the treaty that concluded the Texas Revolution was signed between President ad interim Burnet and General Santa Ana of Mexico. Mason recalled San Luis Island as boasting a beautiful sandy beach and a little land-locked cove which afforded a snug harbour that, so far as he knew, had never been used.

In an absent sort of way, one corner of his mind dwelt on these irrelevant matters, as the mind often will when plagued with a perplexing problem, as he stood gazing into the sunset. He remembered reading that one of the first real battles between Texans and Mexicans was fought at Velasco near San Luis

Island. The farmers and ranchers along the Brazos, resentful because of the high-handed attitude of the Mexican officials, headed by Colonel Domingo Ugartechea, the commander of the Mexican fort, decided on June 25, 1832, to attack Fort Velasco. A schooner lying aground above the fort was dislodged and set afloat, and about forty Texans were placed aboard with ammunition and some artillery. The boat was floated down the river and moored close to the fort. Some seventy Texans, meantime, marched to Velasco by land. The fort was attacked by the land forces and subjected to artillery fire from the schooner, and after a dozen hours of fighting the Mexican garrison surrendered in which was doubtless the first Texas victory over Mexican regulars.

Yes, a section of historical interest to Texans, over there. Mason wondered if Galveston folks ever visited it.

Abruptly he leaned forward, his gaze fixed, as if his eyes rested on something beyond the sunset. He whirled about and headed for the docks and the Island Queen in a hurry.

Dud Gavens and Pete Blake, the Island Queen's skipper, were gloomily sharing a drink when Mason strode up the gangplank.

'Pete,' he said, without preamble, 'you are acquainted with the coast of San Luis Island, aren't you?'

'Sure,' replied the captain, 'been past there

63

lots of times. Why?'

'Then perhaps you recall a little cove to the west, where a ship can lie snug?'

'Uh-huh,' answered Blake. 'On the San Luis Pass. Looks over toward the mouth of the Brazos and Velasco. Why?'

For the second time Mason ignored the skipper's question. 'All right, I want you to cast off in the morning, run the Queen over to San Luis Island and anchor her in the cove,' he said.

His hearers stared at him. 'But blazes!' protested Gavens. 'You don't aim to put on a show over there! There ain't many people live in Velasco and Freeport, the only towns nearby, and they'd hardly row over just to see a show. We wouldn't have the front seats filled.'

'You never mind about the front seats, I'll take care of them,' Mason promised. 'This is Wednesday. What I want you to do is be all set to put on the best performance Saturday night you've ever handled. I'm depending on you. First thing in the morning, Pete. Now I've got some folks to see.' He strode back down the gangplank, leaving the astounded pair staring after him.

Mason proceeded to 'see some folks' without delay. Among them were tug owners and a printer. The following evening, a crowd of lively urchins eager to make a few nickels distributed printed handbills all over Galveston which read, in part :

FREE MOONLIGHT FERRY SERVICE
to
ROMANTIC SAN LUIS ISLAND and
THE SHOWBOAT ISLAND QUEEN
After the Performance, Those who Wish it
Will be Ferried to Velasco, Shrine of Texas
Independence, Where The Treaty Concluding
the Texas Revolution Was Signed.

'It'll be a moonlight night, all right,' Blaine Mason chuckled to Klingman. 'Hope it doesn't rain.'

'Wonder if the notion will catch on?' said Klingman.

'I've a hunch it will,' Mason replied. 'We'll just have to wait and see.'

CHAPTER EIGHT

It didn't rain. And the 'notion' caught on. Early Saturday evening discovered interested and curious town folks streaming to the docks, where they found lines of big lighters fitted up with benches for their accommodation. Two tugs provided motive power.

The moonlight ferry cruise to San Luis Island was voted a huge success and most enjoyable. On the Island Queen, Dud Gavens, the ebullient showman, was inspired by the

65

turn of events. So were the players, and a performance was given that would be talked about for some time to come.

After the last curtain descended, most of the audience decided to visit Velasco before heading back home. They did, much to the profit of Velasco bar and restaurant owners.

Those who attended the Island Queen's opening performance at San Luis Island brought back glowing reports. As a result, the Queen continued to play to capacity crowds and the little town of Velasco prospered.

And in less than two weeks a howl of righteous indignation went up from Galveston waterfront owners of bars, restaurants and dance halls. Formerly, the crowds visiting the Island Queen had paused on the waterfront for drinks, a snack, and perhaps a few dances or a hand or two of cards. Now all that money was going to Velasco. The dock workers had industriously spread the story of why the Queen left Galveston. The owners of the waterfront establishments knew very well who was the author of their woes. Those influential businessmen, who could swing no small number of votes, descended on the Hall like forty hen-hawks on a settin' quail.

'I told you not to tangle with him,' Chauncey Weed said after the air had cleared a little. 'He's got us where the hair is short, and when he pulls, we'll have to dance.'

'I guess we'll have to make peace with the

young devil,' growled Honest John. The others nodded gloomy agreement.

'On his terms,' said Weed.

After considerable debate as to what should be done, a delegation headed by Honest John, high in office, waited for Blaine Mason in Jeth Bixby's waterfront office. Chauncey Weed had been chosen spokesman. He wasted no time.

'All right, Mason, you win,' he said. 'Bring your darned old tub back and we'll give her a clean bill of health.'

Mason rolled and lighted a cigarette before replying. 'Gentlemen,' he said, 'it cost me quite a bit of money to ferry people to San Luis Island and back.'

A moment of dismayed silence followed.

'It's a hold-up!' wailed Honest John.

'Yes,' said Mason, 'but not with an empty gun. When you gentlemen staged your own little hold-up, a while back, you forgot to put cartridges in your shootin' iron. Mine's loaded!'

Mason and the 'statesmen' went into executive session, after which he sent out for drinks which his visitors partook of with evident relish.

'By the way,' he said, 'haven't any of you gentlemen been to see our show? I think you'd really enjoy it, and I'll feel complimented if each of you will accept a season's pass from me.'

'I'll take one,' Chauncey Weed instantly

accepted. 'I'll use it, too. I'm going to see the very first performance after the boat gets back here.'

Results stemming from that impulsive invitation were destined to do things to Blaine Mason's peace of mind.

Back safe in the sanctum of civic government, Honest John suddenly remarked,

'Darn it! In spite of all he's done to us, I like that young feller. Of course we can't allow him to get too uppity, but just the same I like him. Now send for Sam Gulden. I want to talk to that wind spider.'

The conference which followed was an exceedingly uncomfortable one for Sam Gulden, who was blamed by his associates for getting them into the mess. That fanned his anger against Blaine Mason to a white heat of fury.

The Island Queen's return was something in the nature of a gala event. When she steamed into Galveston harbour, gay with flags and coloured bunting, tugs tooted, fog horns bellowed, cheering longshoremen lined the docks.

'We'll hold her here two weeks and then send her to Corpus Christi,' Mason told Caleb Klingman. 'No, I'm not going with her; I've got my hands full here. Jeth Bixby isn't well and I'm taking over for him till he gets better. Might be a good idea for you to go along, though. The fellow you hired to help you with the rooming-house appears to be dependable, and of course I'll be around. Go ahead, it will be a nice trip for you, and I'll feel better with you along to keep an eye on things.'

'Darned if I don't believe I will,' replied Klingman. 'Haven't been anywhere for quite a spell.'

True to his promise, Chauncey Weed attended the first Galveston performance, in Mason's company. Mr. Weed was a bachelor of thirty-five, a lawyer and a good one; his knowledge of the law was only exceeded by his knowledge of how it was to be evaded. Skilled in debate, when he chose to enter it, he was a cultured, polished man of the world, and could be very charming when he wished to be. In appearance he was tall, handsome, distinguished looking. Mason couldn't help liking him. Others who contacted Chauncey Weed were affected in a similar fashion.

There was no doubt but that Mr. Weed enjoyed the show. And when Sharon Grant came on with her songs and dances, he leaned forward in his seat.

'Say!' he exclaimed. 'That girl's got something. She's different. Not the average type of showgirl. Yes, she's out of the ordinary.'

When the number was over, he turned to Mason. 'I'd like to meet that girl,' he said. 'Will you introduce me?'

'Of course,' Mason acceded. After the

performance was over, he did so.

Sharon and Mr. Weed appeared to hit it off together from the start. Weed suggested that they visit one of Galveston's better night spots, favoured by politicians and their ladies. Sharon accepted the invitation eagerly. Mason hesitated, then succumbed to Weed's urging and agreed to go along.

When they reached the *cantina,* Weed steered them to a table occupied by three shrewd-eyed, elderly gentlemen. Mason recognized one as Jim Vane, a councilman. The other two were introduced as Phil Duncan and Ernest Billings. They bowed to Sharon, nodded to Mason.

'Been hearing quite a bit about you, Mr. Mason,' said Duncan. 'Chaunce has been talking you up.'

'Nice of him,' smiled Mason.

'Had to,' chuckled Weed. 'Blaine's a bad man to have against you. If you don't believe it, ask Honest John.'

The others chuckled also, as if enjoying a joke.

'John isn't often caught with his cinches loose,' said Billings, a former cowman, 'but he knows when to tie hard and fast when he doesn't want to let go of something.'

This bit of byplay evidently passed over Sharon's head, for she looked puzzled. Mason, however, thought he understood and wondered just what Honest John had in mind.

He recalled hearing that John's motto was, 'if you can't lick 'em, join 'em, or get 'em to join you.'

Weed ordered drinks. The gentlemen took whisky, Sharon asked for a small glass of wine.

'I seldom drink,' she explained.

'Your complexion attests to that,' Weed said gallantly, and received a smile as his reward.

A really good orchestra started playing. Weed glanced at the dance floor, back to Sharon.

'Would you honour me?' he asked.

'Of course,' she replied. 'I love to dance.'

Chauncey Weed quickly showed that he was a fit partner for even a professional dancer. Admiring glances followed them across the floor. Jim Vane chuckled.

'Make a fine looking couple, don't they?' he said. 'Can't say as I ever saw a finer.'

'You're right,' nodded Billings. 'You know what, I've a feeling Chauncey Weed is hooked at last. Yep, he's smitten. I know that dying-duck-in-a-thunderstorm look. Well, I've a notion he could do worse. She's a mighty purty girl, and looks like a mighty nice one, too.'

'If Weed really wants her, he'll get her,' Jim Vane said with conviction. 'Chaunce has a way with women, wouldn't you say so, Mason?'

'Yes,' Mason conceded gloomily, 'I've a notion he has.'

It was late when they escorted Sharon back to the Island Queen, but Mason and Weed stopped at a waterfront bar for a nightcap before going to bed.

'Mason, I wish to thank you for the opportunity to meet Miss Grant,' the lawyer suddenly said. 'She's a wonderful girl, and I think she's meant for something better than dancing on a showboat.'

'It's an honest living,' Mason replied shortly.

'It is,' Weed readily acceded. 'But with all due respect to your Island Queen, I think she is entitled to something better.'

Mason did not further argue the point. In fact, grudgingly perhaps, he was in accord with Weed.

CHAPTER NINE

Late though it was when he got to bed, Mason had trouble going to sleep that night, something unusual for him. And the following day he was irritable and depressed. Finally he concluded that he needed a few hours off by himself.

Since the very nearly successful attempt on his life, he had curtailed his night walks along the Gulf shore and had turned to another form of relaxation. He would hire a horse at one of the local livery stables, have it ferried across to the mainland and take a long ride over the peaceful range.

The horse he rode, a tall bay with good lines, was rather better than the average livery stable renter and despite his turmoil of spirit, Mason was enjoying the ride.

He followed his usual route, heading north by west until he reached broken ground, then swerving south in a wide circle toward the course of the Intra-coastal Canal and then east to the ferry station.

The sun was low in the west, its almost level rays taking on a reddish tinge when he sighted the low but rugged hills ahead. Already shadows were curdling at their base and their shoulders were swathed in royal purple. Mason rode at a leisurely pace until he was less than a mile from that widening and deepening band of shadow. He had not yet veered to the south when he saw a band of five horsemen bulge from behind a ridge about a thousand yards to the north and west. They altered their course until they were headed directly toward him. He watched their slantwise approach with increasing interest. What the devil were that many riders doing here, he wondered. Here there were no cattle to tend, and there was no town anywhere near to the south and west. Of course it could be but a band of cowhands who had circled around the hills from the northwest, where there were ranches, and were headed for Galveston. If that were so, however, they should be veering more to the east.

In the wild and often lawless coastal region, a lone rider is always a bit suspicious of a group. Years of the Brazos River country had taught Mason to regard warily any such band. There were outlaws in the hill country to the north and west who would murder a man for his horse and what might be in his pockets. He turned his horse's head a bit more to the south, glancing back over his shoulder at the distant group that was steadily drawing nearer. Instantly he saw that they had likewise altered their course. He spoke to the horse and quickened its pace. Another glance told him that the riders from the north had also speeded up.

'Horse,' he told his mount, 'this is beginning to look a bit funny. Suppose you sift sand for a bit and see what those gents back there will do.'

A gentle application of the spurs sent the cayuse forward at a much swifter gait. Mason glanced back and his jaw set grimly. There was no longer any doubt but that he was the quarry the mysterious band had in mind. And the thousand yards had shrunk to little more than seven hundred. He drove his spurs home. The startled horse gave a snort and a bound and went away from there. And at that moment Mason yearned for Amber. The big sorrel, he felt confident, would have quickly shown a clean pair of heels to the pursuit. The riders behind were slowly closing the distance. He glanced back; not more than six hundred yards, now.

Something sang overhead and he ducked instinctively, although the slug didn't pass close. To his ears came the whiplash crack of a distant rifle. He loosened his Colt in its sheath and shook his head. Sixgun against rifles. Not so good! He should have had a Winchester in a saddle boot snugged under his left thigh. But who expected anything like this to happen! Blast it, though, he should have anticipated something of the kind, after what happened out on the jetty. Doubtless his every move had been watched, and his lonely rides across the rangeland provided the very opportunity Sam Gulden and his hellions had hoped for. Well, he was in for it. Nothing to do but try and outrun the devils till he found some place where he could hole up and give battle. He gazed ahead. A mile or so distant something flung back the sunlight in a red shimmer. The railroad tracks! They ran from a deep cut in a ridge that scored the prairie north and south. If he could get into that cut he might be able to make a stand. He urged the bay horse to greater speed, straining his eyes ahead. Beyond the tracks was broken ground, ridges and gulleys and dry washes. There was a place to hole up, if he could just get there before he stopped one of the slugs that were coming alarmingly close. He leaned forward in the saddle and talked to the horse.

The bay responded gallantly, giving his all. But it wasn't enough. Directly ahead, now, were the glinting twin ribbons of the tracks. But the pursuit was coming up fast. Less than five hundred yards separated them from their quarry. A bullet flicked the heel of his boot, nearly knocking his foot from the stirrup. Another burned a streak along the bay's haunch, causing it to give a convulsive bound. Mason steadied, spoke soothingly. A third slug ripped through the sleeve of his shirt but missed the flesh. A hundred yards more and he'd be across the tracks. Maybe the bay had enough left to make it. The tracks were not more than fifty yards distant, now. But he never reached them.

From the cut boomed a great locomotive pulling a seemingly endless string of freight cars. With a bitter curse, Mason jerked the bay to a slithering halt with his nose almost against the rocking boxcars. Above the rumble of the train sounded the triumphant whoops of the pursuit. He was trapped!

There was one remaining slender thread of hope. He whirled the bay and sent him scudding along parallel to the train and as close to the moving cars as he dared. The prairie was level here and there was almost no embankment.

The bay was giving everything, but the cars still whisked past as if he were standing still. Mason's heart sank. Now the pursuit was coming towards him on a slant and swiftly closing the gap. A bullet fanned his cheek with its lethal breath. Then abruptly he realized that the sound of the pounding exhaust had deepened. Directly ahead was a steep grade of nearly a mile in length. The engineer was widening his throttle and dropping his reverse bar down the quadrant, and the train was slowing. The rocking boxcars were now moving but little faster than the bay.

Mason stood in his stirrups, gauged the distance. As the front end of the car came abreast of him, he leaned sideways, seized a grab iron with both hands and kicked his feet free.

The terrific jerk nearly tore his arms from their sockets. One hand lost its hold. He swung wildly by the other, slamming against the side of the car, his fingers slipping. Death was spitting at him from the rifle muzzles charging towards him, reaching up from the spinning wheels. He swung his body around between the two cars, made a frantic clutch at one of the end grab irons, caught it, let it go with his other hand. A moment of frenzied floundering and his feet were on the end sill of the car. The triumphant whoops of the killers changed to yells of baffled fury.

But the grade which had been his salvation was very likely to prove his undoing. The train was slowing more and more. The nose of a speeding horse came into Mason's range of vision. He crouched on the end sill, holding on with his left hand, and drew his gun.

Nearly the whole train was on the grade now, and the engine was not yet over the hump. The horse's neck came into view, his withers. Other heads and necks appeared, then the riders. They gave a whoop as they spotted Mason crouched on the end sill and blazed away at him. But the back of a racing horse is not a good stance for shooting at a moving target. The slugs came close, but he was untouched. He took careful aim, pulled trigger, and missed. A second shot likewise went wild. A slug turned his hat sideways on his head. Another grained the flesh of his left arm. He steadied the barrel of his Colt, squeezed the trigger.

The foremost rider, a wild-eyed, bearded individual, spun sideways from his saddle and thudded to the ground. His horse faltered, stumbled and went down. Another catapulted over it. In an instant the pursuers, storming curses, were thrown into confusion. The slowing train gained on them a bit. Mason stuffed fresh cartridges into the cylinder of his Colt, cocked it, and readied himself for the next onslaught. Two of the devils were down, but three remained, and the labouring locomotive was slowing still more.

Again the heads of horses were coming within the narrow field of his vision, again the riders and again the whistle of lead. Splinters were knocked in his face. The bullets thudded into the side of the car. He fired again and again, until his gun was empty, without results. With frenzied speed he ejected the spent shells.

Abruptly he realized there was nothing to shoot at. From the straining locomotive came a triumphant whistle blast. It was over the hump and rolling down the opposite grade, and the train was picking up speed.

Holstering his gun, Mason sagged against the end of the car. His body was drenched with sweat and he was trembling in every limb. But he was numbly thankful that he was able to sweat and shake at all. Even a slight wound might well have knocked him from his precarious perch and under the grinding wheels. Cautiously he thrust his head around the corner of the car. He was over the hump and the pursuit was nowhere in sight. He laboriously climbed to the top of the car and stretched out on the running board, utterly exhausted from excitement and nervous strain.

Recovering somewhat, he sat up, fumbled the makings from his shirt pocket, and with fingers that still shook a bit managed to roll and light a cigarette. Glancing to the rear of the speeding train, he saw a man making his way towards him across the car tops, doubtless the conductor or rear brakeman of the freight. From the cupola of the caboose, the trainmen could hardly have missed seeing the ruckus.

'What happened, cowboy? Were those hellions trying to kill you?' the man called as he stepped across the opening on to Mason's car. 'Looked to us back in the crummy like they were shooting at you.'

'Well,' Mason replied, 'I don't think they were just playing tag.'

'Some owlhoots from the hills, eh?' said the trainman, pausing beside Mason.

'They came from the hills,' Mason answered.

'You all right?' asked the trainman.

'Yes, now that I've got my breath back,' Mason replied. 'It was a pretty warm go while it lasted.'

'Guess it was,' agreed the trainman. 'Well, come on back to the crummy. We've got hot coffee on the stove. I've a notion you could use a cup about now.'

'I sure could,' Mason accepted gratefully.

Mason got off the freight at Angleton, thanked the trainmen for their hospitality and received hearty wishes for better luck next time. Finding that the only train back to Galveston he could catch would leave the old plantation town late, he signed up for a room at a local hotel and went to bed. He arrived at Galveston before noon the following day and found the livery stable keeper in considerable of a dither.

'Blazes!' he said. 'Was just getting ready to send search parties out to look for you. The horse you hired was waiting at the ferry station this morning, saddled and bridled and looking like he'd been rode hard. You'd better hustle down to Water Street and relieve old Caleb Klingman's mind. I sent word to him and he's fit to be hogtied. Yes, you'd better hustle. He was organizing search parties when I talked to him an hour ago.'

Mason hurried to the waterfront to reassure Klingman, explaining merely in the presence of others that while he wasn't in the hull, the horse had taken a notion to sift sand for home, which was true enough. In private he told Klingman just what happened.

'Gulden again!' declared old Caleb, embellishing the statement with a string of crackling oaths that dealt with Sam Gulden's dubious ancestry, his unsavoury present, and his undoubted fiery future.

'I wouldn't blame you a bit if you walked into that blasted saloon and blew the sidewinder from under his hat,' he concluded venomously.

'Once again, not an iota of proof against Gulden,' Mason replied. 'What happened to me yesterday, and worse, has happened to others. And no matter what I may think, I really don't know if Gulden had anything to do with it. If he was back of it, he came close to filling his loop. I wouldn't have given a busted cartridge for my chances when I was hanging on to that end sill and those devils were throwing lead at me.'

'If your number ain't up, nobody can put it up,' grunted Klingman.

'I guess so,' Mason agreed, 'but I was sure all set to hear the croupier yell, 'You're on the black, and you played the red!'

CHAPTER TEN

'Damn it! You can't kill him!' wailed Sam Gulden. 'The hellions I hired to do the job had him cornered, all set to blow him from under his hat. And what happens? He grabs a freight train going sixty miles an hour and shoots it out with all five of them. Kills one and cripples another. The critter ain't human!'

'I told you to lay off trying to get him shot in the back,' said Long Tommy. 'But you wouldn't listen. After the boys at the Hall gave you the devil for getting them into that showboat mess, you flew off the handle and had to have another go at it. And what did it get you? I'll tell you what it's going to get you, if you keep on with that sort of tactics. Some day Mason is going to walk in here and fill you so full of holes you'll starve to death from leaking your vittles out. Mind what I tell you.'

'He can't prove a thing against me,' Gulden muttered.

Long Tommy regarded him a moment

before replying.

'Sam,' he said, 'you're a good business man, a conniver, and you usually cover your tracks; but you always think in terms of percentages. It's true that Mason couldn't prove anything against you. But Mason knows you were back of two attempts to have him killed. You can shove a man like Mason just so far. All of a sudden he'll bust his cinches and turn on you. Up to now, I'd say, he's been deterred by appreciation of possible consequences. Get him mad enough, though, and he'll throw all that to the winds. And if he does, your life won't be worth a busted cartridge.'

'How about you?' asked Gulden meaningly. Long Tommy proceeded to make one of his few mistakes.

'I'm in the clear,' he replied airily. 'Mason doesn't know I exist. To him I'm just your head bartender who, if he's mixed up in the business, has to go along with you and take orders. Mason wouldn't bother with that sort.'

'I guess you're right,' Gulden said slowly. 'Yes, I guess you're right.' His crafty mind was instantly made up to a course of action. If it looked like a showdown in the offing, he'd make sure that Mason knew just what part Long Tommy played in the business. Maybe he could even shift all the blame on to Long Tommy. He, Gulden, was the one who had to take orders. Long Tommy knew he had been mixed up in some off-colour affairs, not killings, but the sort of thing that wouldn't do a business man in a respectable community any good. He just had to go along with him, although he didn't want to. Yes, that was the notion. As the old saying went, maybe he could kill two birds with one stone. Or arrange so they'd kill each other with a couple of forty-five slugs. Gulden knew that Long Tommy was no slouch with a gun. Might be even better than Mason. And one thing was sure, he was more tricky.

These pleasant thoughts flitted through Gulden's brain and took up a permanent habitation there.

'Yes, I guess you're right,' he repeated. 'Maybe, though, that's all to the good. Mason would have no reason to suspect you and that'll give you an advantage when it comes to working against him. He'll be keeping his eye on me and won't pay you any mind. Guess it would be a good notion for you to handle the business from now on. I'll go along with anything you suggest. Maybe that way we can get results.'

Long Tommy smiled complacently. 'Now you're talking sense,' he said. 'Okay, I'll handle things, and next time there won't be any slip-up.' He paused, his brow puckered. 'Seems to me that blasted showboat ought to give us an opportunity somehow,' he added. 'I'll think on it.'

'That's fine,' said Gulden. 'I'm depending

on you to do the right thing. Well, guess it's time to go to work.' He turned to his desk. Long Tommy stifled a grin.

Before he reached the door, Long Tommy turned and came back to the table. He sat down, poured himself a drink and sipped it while Gulden watched him in inquiring surprise. Long Tommy wiped his lips with the back of his bony hand and leaned forward.

'Sam,' he said, his voice very low, 'there's something I've been turning over in my head for quite a spell now. Something that, if it's handled right, will put us in the driver's seat in this town.'

'What in blazes—' began Gulden. Long Tommy held up his hand for silence.

'You know how important the waterfront is to Galveston,' he continued. 'The prosperity of the town depends on shipping. Now listen close, and don't interrupt until I've finished.' He lowered his voice still more to a hoarse whisper.

Gulden listened, and as the plan unfolded his opaque eyes began to glow. After Long Tommy ceased speaking, he sat silent for some moments, tugging his moustache, stroking the bridge of his nose, evidently going over every detail in his mind. Long Tommy watched him; he could see the wheels turning over. Gulden was calculating possible risks, probable advantages. Long Tommy knew he would not reach a decision until he had convinced himself that he would be in little or no danger, physically or financially. The plan, if it worked out, promised money, and money was a controlling factor with Sam Gulden.

Finally Gulden spoke. 'I've a notion it'll work,' he said slowly. 'Yes, I believe it will work. And I know just the man to handle it. He's over at Port Arthur right now, stirring up trouble. I'll send him a wire tonight. But Mason has to be gotten out of the way before he moves. Those blasted dock wallopers will eat out of Mason's hand, but with him out of the way, they can be manipulated. They're just a bunch of sheep, most of them, and will follow a leader into the Gulf, once you get them roused up proper. But Mason is the stumbling block. He's got to be removed if there's any hope of this thing working out. And we don't seem to have much luck eliminating him.'

'Because of your blundering crudeness, once you lose your temper,' reminded Long Tommy. 'I'm beginning to get a notion how Mason can be taken care of, and maybe a little luck will play into my hands to make it easier. Call in your man and we'll move just as soon as we're assured Mason won't be around to gum the works. Okay?'

'Okay,' said Gulden.

This time the two schemers grinned at each other.

CHAPTER ELEVEN

When he entered the office Friday morning of the second week, with the Island Queen due to sail for Corpus Christi after the coming Saturday night performance, Mason got an agreeable surprise. Jeth Bixby was at his desk.

'I'm feeling fine,' he answered Mason's surprised greeting. 'Doctor says I'm all set to go back to work. Now you can make the trip with your darn show-boat to Corpus Christi. It would do you good. You've earned a vacation.'

Mason hesitated, then quickly arrived at a decision. 'Darned if I don't believe I will, if you're sure you're okay to handle the chore here,' he said. 'I think I can stand a change of scene for a few days.'

With directions that they relieve Bixby of as much work as possible, Mason informed his assistants on the docks of his decision, and the word quickly got around and was picked by interested ears.

There was a half moon in the sky and the air was still balmy when the Island Queen steamed out of Galveston harbour and headed west. After seeing that everything was shipshape, Blaine Mason walked to the bow and stood leaning against the rail and gazing across the dark water. Once again the path of the moonbeams stretched before him. But tonight no dreams walked the silvery trail.

Mason smiled at the fantasy, but there was little mirth in his smile. How many countless thousands throughout the ages had stood as he stood, he wondered, and gazed as he gazed, and had grown sad in the midst of beauty. He had watched Chauncey Weed say goodnight to Sharon, bowing over her hand with courtly grace, and he had felt awkward and uncouth by contrast. She had lifted her little flower-like face to him, and her lips had murmured something.

Then abruptly he realized he was no longer alone. She was beside him, leaning on the rail, gazing wide-eyed at the path of the moonbeams. And suddenly the shimmering way was filled with dancing, laughing shapes that can only be seen by two!

'Blaine,' she said, 'I have something to tell you. Tonight Mr. Weed proposed—'

'Yes?' Mason interrupted, his lips dry. 'And I suppose you accepted? Well, I've a notion he'll make a good husband. He—'

A dimple showed at the corner of Sharon's red mouth; she seemed to be struggling with inward laughter.

'Oh, it was not so serious as that,' she interrupted in turn. 'He proposed that I leave the Island Queen for a job of singing and dancing in a big dining place at Houston in which he owns an interest. He said, which was nice of him, that my talents are wasted on a showboat.'

'The devil he did!' Mason gulped, almost incoherent in his relief. 'What did you tell him?'

'I thanked him for the offer and told him I wouldn't leave the Queen.'

'Why?'

'Oh, I like it here—the constant change, the excitement. And I like the people I work with.'

'You could doubtless make more money at the Houston place.'

Sharon shrugged daintily. 'Perhaps,' she conceded, 'but I'm doing all right as it is. And I'm not angling for a raise,' she added with a smile.

'Just the same I think you have one coming,' he said. 'In fact, I think the whole troupe deserves one. They're doing a bang-up job, and business is good.'

'It will be appreciated,' she replied. 'They're not all situated as I am. Some of them have others beside themselves to look after.'

'Do you ever get tired of looking after yourself?' he asked.

Sharon hesitated. 'I really can't say that I do,' she said. 'But I suppose it would be comforting to have somebody to look after me.'

'I'm sure you will have, sooner or later,' he said.

'Perhaps, but sometimes I'm not too sure,' she answered. 'Well, it's time I was in bed;

early rehearsal tomorrow. Goodnight, Mr. Mason.'

Mason remained standing by the rail, gazing over the planet-powdered floor of tossing water. He was more than a little puzzled at Chauncey Weed's action. Gradually, however, it became obvious—his own conclusion—what Weed had in mind: Get the girl away from her associates, to where she wouldn't know anybody, where he, Weed, would be her only real acquaintance. She would naturally turn to him as a friend in a strange environment. Yes, that was it. Chauncey Weed enjoyed a reputation of being a shrewd article. That was just the course of action his subtle mind could be counted on to evolve.

Mason went to bed, but getting to sleep was another matter. He would doze for a while and then wake up. The night was warm, the cabin stuffy, and he was plagued by thoughts that were only partially lucid but damnably persistent. After several aggravating hours he gave it up for the time being. He slipped on a shirt and a pair of Levis and, not bothering to don his boots or buckle on his gun, went out on to the dark deck. He made his way to the rail near the bow and leaned against it even as he had earlier in the night. Overhead the false dawn fled ghost-like across the sky; daylight wasn't far off. But now the moon had set and the night was very dark.

Abruptly he sensed movement behind him.

As he half turned, a shadowy figure loomed on either side. Before he could speak or make a move, hands gripped him. An upward heave and he was over the rail, rushing downward through space, the black water leaping up to meet him. He gave one strangled yell before he submerged.

When he broke surface, the tall side of the Island Queen was sliding past. He swam frantically away from the ship lest he be sucked into the churning propeller. He shouted again and again, but there was no response from the ship. Another moment and her stern lights were dimming into the distance.

Blaine Mason was in trouble and he knew it. He was a good swimmer, but a swim of unknown distance through the choppy waters of the Gulf was an appalling prospect. He estimated the Queen had covered some sixty or seventy miles since leaving Galveston Island, which should place him somewhere in the neighbourhood of Matagorda Peninsula, but he hadn't the slightest notion how far out in the Gulf he was. It could easily be many miles, for the skipper would not be likely to hug the dangerous Texas shore which was a rough and rocky coast with treacherous reefs. Nor could he hope for any help from the ship; the Island Queen was a big boat and his absence would hardly be noticed until many hours had passed. He blessed his lucky stars that he was not encumbered by his gun and his boots. His thin shirt and Levis weren't much of a drag. Perhaps he'd be able to stay afloat long enough to reach land or be picked up by a fishing boat. His best bet would be to try to swim to the shore. Which, he grimly admitted, was about like betting on an incompleted inside straight from a stripped deck.

Such were the thoughts that flashed through his brain as he paddled to keep afloat, husbanding his strength for the almost hopeless pull to the coast as soon as it was light enough for him to see where he was going.

A veil of cloud hid the stars and the dark was absolutely stygian. But gradually a spot of grey showed in one quarter of the sky. Huge misty shapes moved over the surface of the water like ghosts of long-forgotten dawns. They were vapours rising from their watery bed to greet the sun. The spot of grey widened, turned to rose and scarlet. Bars of light sprang up across the eastern sky, burned crimson, deepened to molten flame.

Mason heaved a deep sigh of relief and began to swim. Now there was no doubt as to direction. All he had to do was keep that blazing dawn on his right and he was headed for the Texas shore.

Only there was no shore to be seen. Lifting his head as much as he could, his limited range of vision covered nothing but tossing blue water. Despair tugged at his heart. He couldn't keep it up much longer. Already his arms were aching, and there was a suspicion of cramp in his right leg. And the water, while far from being icy, was still cold enough to send a chill into his bones. He lifted his head again, craned his neck. Nothing but the unbroken surface of the Gulf. He must have miscalculated the distance the Island Queen had covered; he was further east of Matagorda Peninsula than he thought. And that jut of land was his sole hope. A forlorn hope. It didn't matter much any more. He was so tired. His arms and legs still moved mechanically, but a cold numbness was coiling about his brain. The blue water was turning black. The brightness of the sun was dimming.

He went under, fought his way back to the surface, retching from the salt water he had swallowed. Wearily he raised his head for one last look at the sky that was still faintly blue.

CHAPTER TWELVE

Something drifted across his range of vision, something alien, different from the blackening waters. He strained his eyes for a better look. Abruptly his vision cleared a little, enough to realize what that thing of glittering white must be. A sail!

The strange and unexplainable urge that makes the quivering clay seek to grasp the escaping soul took over, told him what to do. He raised his arm and waved it frantically. From his tortured lungs came a hoarse shout. A trim little boat carrying a singularly large sail for her size was tacking toward him.

Not close enough! She'd pass to the north! Again, with the last strength of despair, he waved his leaden arm. Again that rasping bellow sounded from his throat.

The boat came about, hung in the wind. The wind spilled out of the sail and she surged straight for where he struggled to keep afloat. The sail came rattling down. He could see a figure fighting the helm. Then the wooden hull rasped his side. A hand reached down. Fingers clutched his wrist. With his free hand he got a grip on the gunwale, and as the boat dipped to the strain, flung one leg over. A moment of exhausting struggle and he was sprawled across the thwarts, retching and gasping, red flashes storming before his eyes.

The sail was going up. It banged and bellied as the wind filled it. 'Lie still until I lash the tiller,' said a voice.

Mason obeyed. He was too exhausted to do otherwise. He closed his eyes a moment to shut out the unbearable flashes. He opened them and looked up.

A girl was standing over him. He absently noted that she was a rather tall girl with great dark eyes and, in startling contrast, hair the colour of daffodils in the sun.

'Where in the world did you come from?' she asked.

'Over the side,' he replied with a wan grin.

'So I gathered,' she said. 'Over what side—a fishing boat?'

'The Island Queen,' he answered.

The big eyes widened a little. 'Oh, the showboat. I was on her when she tied up at San Luis Island. Must have been her lights I saw just before I put out from shore. I like to sail into the sunrise.'

'Darn lucky for me you do,' he said, and managed to prop his head on one hand.

She seemed to study him for a moment. 'You look like a cowhand,' she remarked.

'I was once,' he replied.

'You were working on the boat?'

Mason essayed a sitting position before replying. His strength was returning and he was feeling a lot better.

'Nope,' he said, 'I own the blasted thing. She had a reputation for being a bad luck piece. I'm beginning to believe the hoodoo's still working.'

Her eyes widened still more. 'Why, you must be Mr. Blaine Mason!' she exclaimed. 'You were pointed out to me when I visited the boat and saw the show. You looked different.'

'A little less like a drowned rat, I guess,' he remarked.

'Can't say about the rat part, but you sure look half drowned,' she said.

'I was considerable more than half when you came along,' he admitted. 'And it's thanks to you that I'm not at the bottom of the Gulf right now.'

'Glad I was able to help,' she replied cheerfully. 'Now you just take it easy. I'm going to bring her about and head for the shore. You can stand some hot coffee and food and clothes. I have a horse at the landing and he'll pack double. Only a short ride to the house.'

'Just a minute,' he said as she turned to unlash the tiller, 'do you mind telling me your name.'

'It's Cora Walters,' she answered. 'My father owns the Bradded L ranch. He's about your size and I guess his clothes will fit you fairly well.'

Skimming along before a freshening wind, the little boat made good time. In less than an hour they sighted land. Another half hour and the girl ran her smoothly into a little sheltered cove where a small dock had been constructed. She deftly looped a mooring line into place, lowered and furled the sail.

'All set to go,' she said. 'There's my horse over there, filling up with grass. My rig's in the leanto; I'll get it. You take it easy till I saddle up; you still look pretty well worn out.'

Mason, who had been drowsing with the

aftermath of extreme exhaustion, really took a good look at his rescuer for the first time. She wasn't hard to look at. There was a litheness and curves to her figure that even Levis and blue cotton shirt much like his own could not conceal. Her complexion was the clear bronze that only the pure blonde colouring can achieve from wind and sun. There was a singular brilliance to her dark eyes and glints of gold in her yellow hair. The glints were really almost reddish, he dreamily decided. Altogether, she was a good deal of an eyeful.

With swift ease, the rig went into place on the big blue moros. The girl swung into the saddle.

'Up behind me,' she directed. 'Not far to go.'

It wasn't. Less than two miles had been covered when, rounding a grove, they sighted a big ranchhouse set on a rise. Bunkhouse and other buildings, Mason noted, were in excellent repair. As he could see, numerous cattle grazed on the fine rangeland. Evidently Mr. Walters was a man of substance and bountifully endowed with this world's goods. As they neared the house, a big old man stood up on the wide veranda and waved a greeting.

'Now what the devil you got?' he demanded.

Cora slipped to the ground, tied the moros securely to the morning breeze, and hauled Mason forward by the hand.

'Dad, this is Mr. Blaine Mason who owns

the Island Queen,' she introduced. 'I fished him out of the Gulf. Mr. Mason, this is my father, Judson Walters.'

'She's always packing something home,' Walters said as he shook hands. 'A while back it was a crippled wolf cub. He grew into a fine dog. Around somewhere. And back in the kitchen a pigeon with a busted wing is struttin' around, peckin' the cat on the head and getting into everybody's way. How are you, Mr. Mason? Were you taking an early morning swim?'

'Something of that sort, rather against my will,' Mason said. He liked Judson Walters' looks at once.

'Come on in,' chuckled Walters. 'I'll root you out some duds. They ought to fit you pretty well—we look to be about a size. Then you can tell me how you came to be maverickin' around in the Gulf this time of day. Cora, show him to the first room at the head of the stairs while I rake up the clothes, and tell the cook to rustle his hocks and get coffee and a surrounding of chuck ready. Scoot along, Mason.'

A little later, the salt washed from his face, his thick tawny hair neatly combed, and garbed in clean shirt and Levis and boots that fitted fairly well, Mason descended to the big, tastefully furnished living-room to find Walters alone there.

'Here's the makin's,' said the rancher,

shoving tobacco and papers across the table to his guest. 'Reckon you could stand a drag or two about now. Coffee and something to eat will be ready in a jiffy.'

Mason thankfully rolled and lighted a brain tablet. Walters regarded him through the blue haze of his pipe. Mason arrived at a quick decision. He felt it best to tell his host just what did happen and proceeded to do so. When he paused, Walters eyed him thoughtfully.

'Tell you what I'll bet,' he said. 'I'll bet you that when you get to Corpus Christi you'll find a couple of somebodies missing. You any notion who it was tossed you in the drink?'

Mason mentioned the two pseudo seamen the captain had hired the day before. Walters nodded his understanding. 'Yep, those would very likely have been the sidewinders, and you'll find they trailed their twine soon as the boat tied up. Son, what was back of it?'

Again Mason arrived at a decision. He proceeded to tell Walters the whole story, beginning with the drugging and subsequent robbing in the Crystal Bar. Walters listened with interest and without comment until Mason had finished. Then he said,

'I know Sam Gulden. Know that ganglin' head barkeep of his, too, the jigger they call Long Tommy. Name's Hordle. Leastwise that's what he calls himself in this section. He's a killer type or I never saw one. Owns half the business.'

Mason stared. 'The devil he does!' he exclaimed. 'I never heard that. Always thought Gulden was the sole owner.'

'It ain't generally known,' said Walters. 'But I happen to be a director of the Galveston National. The Crystal Bar had occasion to deal with the bank, and its business set-up had to be revealed before they could get what they wanted. Such matters aren't talked about by the bank, of course. I wouldn't be telling you if I didn't think it was to your interest to know. Hordle—Long Tommy—is the man you want to watch. I've a notion Gulden is just a sneaky thief—didn't favour him much from the beginning—but Hordle is dangerous, as it appears you've had occasion to remark.'

'They've tried the land and the water,' Mason observed grimly. 'Reckon if I sprouted wings they'd try to bring me down from the air.'

'Quite likely,' agreed Walters. 'You see, the hellions don't know for sure just how much you know, but suspect it's too much for their comfort. Chances are they suspect you're just biding your time before dropping a loop on them. So they're out to remove you, and if you don't watch out, they'll do just that. Three tries, eh? Keep your eye open for a fourth.'

'What they don't know,' Mason said, 'is that I really haven't a thing on them, only suspicion.'

'The Scriptures say, "The guilty flee when no man pursueth." Walters observed sententiously. 'And a cornered rat is a dangerous rat. Well, the cook's bellerin' for us to come and get it. Where's that maverickin' tomboy of mine? Guess she's primpin' a bit. Come on, let's eat. She'll be along when she gets ready.'

Mason realized that he was ravenous and proceeded to do full justice to the ample meal set before him. Cora arrived shortly. She had changed to something distinctly feminine which, Mason thought, to employ the conventional phrase, was very becoming. However, he reflected, overalls had also been becoming with Cora inside them. Cora Walters didn't need extraneous adornment to make her attractive.

'I should be figuring a way to get to Corpus Christi,' Mason remarked after they had finished eating and were smoking in the living room. 'By now they will surely have missed me and be wondering what happened. Caleb Klingman will very quickly decide it was something off-coloured and he'll be fit to be tied.'

'Tell you what,' suggested Walters. 'I'll have one of the boys ride to Bay City to the north of here and send the boat a wire letting them know you're okay. Tomorrow, if you want to, you can catch a train at Bay City for Corpus Christi. I figure you'll be better without a long jaunt today. How's that?'

'That'll be fine,' Mason accepted gratefully. He glanced at Cora as he spoke. She smiled, and her long and dark lashes drooped a trifle.

'Write out a message,' said Walters. 'You know what you want to say. Paper and pen and ink in the drawer at your elbow.'

Mason wrote a brief message assuring Klingman of his safety but explaining nothing. He debated whether he should mention the two 'seamen' he suspected as the authors of the outrage, but concluded not to.

Walters proceeded to dispatch the message without delay. Mason, his concern over old Caleb relieved, relaxed and enjoyed Cora's very charming company. He was not at all averse when she suggested a ride together.

'Being pitched over a ship's rail has recompenses, after all,' he chuckled. 'I don't regret the incident one bit. In fact, if I knew where to locate them, I think I'd send those two hellions a note of thanks.'

Cora blushed prettily. 'That was nicely said, even though you don't mean it,' she replied. 'Come on, let's get the horses. I'll have the wrangler pick out a nice gentle one for you as a reward.'

The big roan the wrangler brought around, along with Cora's moros, did not look particularly gentle, but he did show indications of speed and endurance.

Cora set the pace, the tall moros fleeting

across the prairie like the shadow of a cloud. The roan apparently had no difficulty keeping up with him, but its gait was less smooth. He talked soothingly to the horse, caressing its neck with his slim fingers. Cora's glance registered approval.

'You have a way with horses,' she said. 'He'd run his heart out for you.'

She eased the moros as she spoke and they rode on side by side. The day had fulfilled the promise of the morning. The late summer rangeland was flooded with golden sunshine. The grasses were emerald billows tipped with the amethyst of the ripening heads, and the deeper hollows were flaunting their crimson banners and their yellow beacons of flame.

CHAPTER THIRTEEN

They rode slowly on the return trip. The sun had set and the shadows were long when they reached the ranchhouse.

' 'Bout time you were getting back,' said Walters. 'I'm starving to death. Wash up and let's eat 'fore I tumble over from weakness.'

Mason and Walters were enjoying an after-supper smoke when the hand to whom had been entrusted the chore of sending the telegram to Corpus Christi rode in with an answer from Caleb Klingman. Mason chuckled and passed the message to Walters, who also chuckled when he read, 'You'll be the death of me yet.'

'I've a notion the old gent thinks a lot of you,' he remarked as he handed back the paper.

'He's sort of a second father to me,' Mason replied. 'Caleb's all right.'

'I'd like to meet him,' said Walters. 'Well, here comes Cora; been primpin' again. I'm going to bed. You young folks can sit up all night and jabber if you're of a mind to, but an old feller like me needs his rest.'

Blaine Mason would long remember that evening in the living-room of the Bradded L ranchhouse. It had been quite a while since he enjoyed the company of a cultured, educated, and very charming woman. When he went to bed in his comfortable room he was in a quite different mood than when, not many hours before, he had glowered gloomily at the Island Queen's forefoot snoring steadily through the flame tipped waters of the Gulf.

But just the same, Sharon Grant's piquant little face kept drifting past the range of his subconscious vision. Oh, the devil! She belonged to another man. The cure for a woman is another woman. And the one that just a short while before had told him good-night in a soft, sweet voice should make a man forget all else. Only, darn it, he couldn't forget.

The following morning, Judson Walters had

a surprise for Mason.

'Tell you what,' he said. 'We've decided to ride to Bay City with you and catch a train for Corpus Christi. I want to see your show.'

'Fine!' Mason applauded. 'I'm sure you'll enjoy it, and it will be a great pleasure to have you with us.' He glanced at Cora who lowered her lashes demurely.

'Thanks for talking your father into it,' he said when Walters had left to prepare the horses.

'What makes you think I talked him into it?' she asked.

'I don't know, but I hope you did,' he returned.

Sharon Grant was waiting at the head of the gangplank when Mason escorted his guests aboard the Island Queen. She gracefully acknowledged the introductions, shot Mason a penetrating glance, but asked no questions. The colour in her cheeks deepened a little and her eyes were starry with something that glinted on their dark lashes.

'Take them around, Shay, and show them the sights,' Mason directed. 'I'll be with you in a jiffy—want to change clothes.'

Old Caleb came hurrying forward at that moment and was introduced.

'And if it hadn't been for Miss Cora, who fished me out of the Gulf, I'd very likely have stayed among the missing,' Mason explained.

'Ma'am,' said Caleb, 'you've sure put us all

105

heavy in your debt, mighty, mighty heavy, and there ever comes a chance to pay it off, we'll be there with bells on, won't we, Sharon?'

'We will,' the little dancer agreed with finality.

Klingman accompanied Mason to the cabin. 'Now, just what did happen?' he asked after they were inside with the door shut.

Mason told him. Caleb swore sulphurously. 'Gulden again, eh?' he said.

'I suppose so,' Mason replied wearily. 'I have something to tell you about him later, something I learned from Walters. First, though, are these two supposed-to-be-seamen Blake hired just before we left Galveston still around?'

'I don't know, but I did hear Blake cussing this morning about being short-handed again,' Klingman answered.

'Get Blake and bring him here,' Mason directed.

Klingman hurried from the cabin and in a little while reappeared with the captain in tow.

'The swabs jumped ship soon as we tied up,' Blake replied to Mason's question.

'Can you recall what they looked like?' Mason asked.

'Scrubby looking pair,' Blake answered. 'Both big fellers. One had a scar across the bridge of his nose. Didn't notice much about the other. Both needed a shave and looked like the morning after. Why?'

Mason repeated what he told Klingman. Blake proceeded to far surpass Klingman's finest efforts at profanity. Mason listened with admiration. Never before had he the faintest conception of the breadth and depth and height of a ship captain's objurgatory powers.

'But cussing won't help much,' he said, when Blake paused for breath. 'They're gone, and the chances are we'll never lay eyes on them again. They figured their chore was done, properly, and trailed their twine. I'm beginning to wish I'd stayed under cover for a while. Then maybe the two hellions who handed them the chore might have tipped their hand.'

'Two?' asked Klingman. 'You mean there's somebody else in on it besides Sam Gulden?'

Mason recounted what he had learned from Judson Walters concerning Long Tommy Hordle's partnership in the Crystal Bar.

'Well, I'll be hanged!' sputtered Klingman. 'Long Tommy! I remember that sidewinder. Walters is right, he's the killer type, a long sight more dangerous than Gulden, I'd say. So he's in on it, too. But darn it, Blaine, this can't go on forever. Something's got to be done.'

'But what?' asked Mason. 'I've wracked my brains for a solution and can't hit on one.'

Captain Blake looked bewildered. 'What's this all about?' he asked.

'I think you'd better tell him, Blaine,' suggested Klingman.

Mason did so. Blake swore even better than before. 'My advice,' he concluded, 'is that we walk in that rumhole with a brace of shotguns and do the community a favour.'

'The idea appeals,' Mason conceded, 'but I'm afraid we can't risk it till we get some proof.'

'I think I'll have a little talk with Chauncey Weed,' Klingman said thoughtfully. 'I figure he'll be showing up here before long. If anybody can get something on a sidewinder, he can. Yes, I'm going to have a talk with Weed.'

'All right,' Mason agreed. 'Don't see how it can do any harm. Weed's smart, and he'll keep a tight latigo on his jaw. That goes for you, too, Pete. Don't mention what we told you.'

'I won't,' Blake promised, 'and from now on I'm going to follow you around like a pet dog. I've got a sawed-off six-gauge shotgun I'm going to strap under my arm. It packs fourteen buckshot to the cartridge.'

'And if you cut loose with that baseburner you'll blow the ship out of the water,' Mason declared with conviction. 'I never saw but one six-gauge; muzzles looked like twin nail-kegs.'

'She's a beauty,' said Blake complacently, 'and when she goes after something, she gets it. What's left has to be picked up with a blotter.'

Mason rolled a cigarette and turned to the door. 'I'm going out and hunt up the folks,' he said. 'Getting close to time for Sharon to make ready for the performance.'

He found Sharon and Cora standing by the starboard rail, deep in conversation. Walters had wandered off somewhere with Dud Gavens.

'So there you are!' Sharon greeted. 'Was beginning to think you'd fallen into the water again. You'll have to look after Cora. I've got to get in costume.'

With a wave of her hand she trotted away. Cora watched her go, a thoughtful expression on her face.

'I think,' she said slowly, 'that she's the prettiest girl I ever laid eyes on. No wonder you're so interested in the showboat business.'

'An interest in her would be just a waste of time,' Mason replied gloomily.

Cora glanced at him from the corners of her eyes and smiled.

That night the Island Queen played to capacity. Among those present was the Mayor of Corpus Christi, who made a point of looking up Mason after the performance.

'Glad to have you with us, Mr. Mason,' he said as they shook hands. 'You've got folks all excited. Your show was excellent. I enjoyed it very much and look forward to seeing another performance. By the way, Honest John—nobody ever calls him anything else—from Galveston mentioned you when he was visiting me the other day. He appears to hold you in high regard, although he says you're a good deal of a darn nuisance, always setting something by the ears.'

'I don't mean to be,' Mason laughed. 'It was nice of him to remember me.'

'He's a good man to have as a friend,' said the Mayor. 'And anybody he looks upon as a friend is a friend of mine. Goodnight, Mr. Mason. If I can ever be of assistance to you, don't hesitate to call on me. I mean it.'

Mason accompanied Cora and her father to the hotel where they would spend the night. In the lobby, the rancher shook hands.

'We had a swell time, son,' he said. 'Enjoyed every minute of it. You'll come to see us some time? The Bradded L isn't so far from Galveston.'

'I certainly will,' Mason promised. He glanced at Cora.

'Yes, please do,' she said. 'And I'm going to make Dad take me to Galveston soon after the boat goes back there.'

'Look me up soon as you arrive,' Mason said. 'You can always find me on the docks or the boat. I'll be looking for you.'

'We will,' Walters said. 'Good night, son.'

Mason walked up the gangplank and across the deck to the starboard rail where he found a small figure gazing across the starlit waters.

'Why, hello, Shay,' he said. 'You're staying up late.'

'Yes,' she replied without turning her head. 'There is no moon, but the night is beautiful.'

'It is,' Mason nodded. 'Well, what do you think of her?'

'She's nice,' Sharon answered. 'I like her. She's beautiful, and stately, too. Don't you think so?'

'Why yes, I guess she is,' Mason conceded.

'Her father is very wealthy, isn't he?'

'So I gather.'

'And she's an only child?'

'I believe she is,' Mason replied. 'What are you getting at, Shay?'

'Nothing, except I'd say she'll make some man a wonderful wife.'

'I don't doubt it,' Mason agreed. 'Especially if he happens to be a city man. She wants to live in a city.'

'Don't you?'

'Nope,' he replied. 'I've tried it. I even get a bit weary of Galveston at times, and after all, Galveston is just a big frontier town with the rangeland right in its back yard.'

'I see,' Sharon said slowly.

'You see what?'

'That your path is likely to be beset by difficulties.'

Mason stared, but could make nothing of her face in the gloom.

'Now what the devil do you mean by that?' he demanded.

'It's up to you to find the answer,' she said. 'Good night, Blaine.'

'Good night, Shay. See you tomorrow.'

He gazed after her departing form and shook his head. In his cabin a little later, he glowered at an unimpressed bulkhead.

'Why,' he asked exasperatedly, 'do women always have to talk in riddles?'

If the bulkhead knew the answer, it kept it to itself.

CHAPTER FOURTEEN

Five days later, during which time he saw very little of Sharon Grant who seemed to purposely avoid him, Mason received a telegram from Jeth Bixby. The terse message was cryptic and, he felt, a bit ominous—'Come back as soon as you can.'

After saying a hurried goodbye to Sharon and Caleb Klingman, Mason caught the first train for Galveston.

'I don't know what's up, but there must be something wrong or Jeth would not have sent so urgent a message,' he told them. 'I'd better not waste any time getting there. See you soon.'

It was late when Mason reached the Galveston waterfront, but a light burned in Bixby's office and he found the labour contractor busy at his desk.

'Hello, so you made it fast,' said Bixby. 'Take a chair till I finish this time sheet. I'll be with you in a minute.'

Mason sat down and rolled a cigarette. He smoked in silence while Bixby's pen scratched down figures.

'Well, what's the matter?' he asked when Bixby shoved the papers aside and looked up.

'I don't know exactly what, for sure,' Bixby replied. 'But one thing is sure for certain, somebody is kicking for trouble.'

'Trouble? What do you mean?'

'I mean that all the dockers appear to be getting together,' Bixby replied. 'It started over at the other end of the waterfront and has been spreading.'

'They have a perfect right to organize and to bend their efforts toward securing better wages and working conditions,' Mason said. 'That's the American prerogative and I'm wholeheartedly in favour of it.'

'So am I, as you very well know,' replied Bixby. 'But this thing is different. It seems to be a sort of hate-gospel that's being preached to the workers by agitators who have all of a sudden appeared from nowhere. They are being told that they are slaves, that the shippers and others are rolling in luxury based on their labour, and that they are being thrown a pittance. That's the line that's being handed out, along with thinly veiled exhortations to violence. They're being told, indirectly but effectively, that only by the destruction of the property of the greedy extortionists can they hope to get justice. That, they are told, will bring the leeches to their knees.'

'The devil you say!' exclaimed Mason. 'When did this start?'

'The day after you arrived in Corpus Christi, so far as I've been able to gather,' Bixby answered. 'Of course there may have been an underground movement before, but that's the date they came out into the open, or so I've been given to understand.'

'Interesting,' Mason commented thoughtfully. 'Are our boys affected?'

'No, at least not so far,' Bixby replied. 'Thanks largely to you, our gang consists of the best and most intelligent workers on the docks. They can't see the thing, but they're puzzled as to what it's all about, and pressure is being brought to bear on them in a subtle way. It was from them that I first learned of the business. Several of them came and told me. They thought I should know. And they asked when you'd be back. Said the Old Man might be needed bad if things got out of control. I figured they were right and sent you that telegram.'

'They probably were,' Mason agreed. 'And you say there has been no demand for higher wages or changes in working conditions?'

'As I said before, that doesn't seem to be the line,' answered Bixby. 'So far as I can learn, there has been no mention made of wages or working conditions or organization to better both, just rabble-rousing propaganda. That may come later, of course. The whole thing could be a build-up for such demands, but somehow I don't think so. The speakers just bear down on what they call the injustice that's being done the workers.'

'I see,' Mason said. 'The sort of thing that inflames ignorant minds and incites to violence even though the perpetrators haven't the slightest notion why they're doing what they are. Folks can get drunk on rhetoric as easily as on whisky.'

'That's right,' agreed Bixby. 'What do you think of the business, Blaine?'

'I don't know what to think, yet,' Mason answered. 'But one thing has occurred to me. It might be an attempt on the part of somebody to gain control of the waterfront.'

'Yes?'

'Yes, by building up to a general strike with demands that can't be met, followed by violence. Then, when the time's ripe, by sliding in their own men to break the strike and take over. That sort of thing has been done before elsewhere. Could be here. Seems a bit far-fetched, but I consider it worth thinking on.'

'You could be right,' Bixby agreed.

Mason stood up and pinched out his cigarette. 'Well, it's nearly midnight and I'm going to bed,' he said. 'Tomorrow I'll have a talk with the boys and see what I can learn. Good night, Jeth.'

The next morning Mason talked with some of the leading men of the gang. They confirmed what Bixby told him the night before. He pondered what he had heard for some minutes and arrived at a decision.

'Get all the boys of our gang together and bring them here,' he directed.

Quickly the order was obeyed. Mason looked at the sea of expectant faces.

'You know what I want to talk to you about,' he prefaced his remarks. 'First of all, I want to say that if this movement of which I've been told is a legitimate attempt to properly organize and unionize the dock workers, I'm for it. But so far as I've been able to learn, it's nothing of the sort.' He paused, then repeated what he told Bixby, that he suspected the object of the movement was to give somebody control of the waterfront who would supplant the present crews with men of his own choosing.

'Wouldn't be a bit surprised if you've got the right of it, boss,' said a big fellow in the front rank. 'Looks a bit like that to me. You know, something of the sort happened back in '83. Wasn't as bad as this looks to be and was handled different, but just the same, when it was over, a lot of fellers found themselves without jobs. We don't want anything like that to happen now.'

'We don't,' Mason agreed. 'And I don't see any reason why it should happen. You know that when you have a grievance of any kind, you can always come to me and I'll listen.'

'That's so,' shouted several voices. 'The Old Man's all right.'

'Thank you,' Mason said. 'And you know also that Mr. Bixby's books are always open for a selected committee to examine. You know he puts his cards on the table, shows you just how he stands and what he can do and can't do.'

'That's right, too.'

'So that's how the situation stands,' Mason concluded. 'I'll repeat, I'm all for organization and properly conducted unions, but this business looks sort of off-colour to me. I hope none of you boys will be taken in by it, if it turns out to be what I've been told. I'm going to do a bit of investigating on my own hook and let you know what I learn.'

'We're with you, boss,' the workers shouted. 'And if it comes to trouble, we'll be right with you then, too, and we know you'll be with us till the last cow comes home. Hurrah for the Old Man!'

The cheers were given with a will and the longshoremen trooped back to work.

'I don't think we need worry about our boys,' Mason told Bixby. 'And it's up to us to back them to the limit.'

'That's just what we'll do,' declared the contractor.

'And tonight I'm going to attend one of those meetings you told me about and try and get the lowdown on this business,' Mason said.

'Okay,' Bixby agreed, albeit a bit dubiously. 'But be careful. You might run into trouble.'

'I'll chance it,' Mason replied. 'Incidentally, I'll take one of the boys with me so we can check on each other's impressions.'

'A good notion,' nodded Bixby. 'Maybe you'd better take a dozen.'

'That would be asking for trouble,' Mason answered with a smile. 'The boys aren't exactly the meek and forbearing sort, and if something didn't go to suit them, they might start a brannigan. I can control one, but not a dozen when they get their mad up.'

Mason did not choose one of his assistants as a companion but a big fellow named Terence Mulraney who, among other things, had once worked as a cowhand and who was in the nature of a spokesman for the workers.

'There's going to be a meeting over at the other end of the waterfront,' Mulraney said. 'Over there is a sort of headquarters for the bunch that's stirring up things; there'll be talking.'

They made their way to where a dense crowd of longshoremen were assembled. A speaker's stand had been erected, lighted by flaring kerosene torches. From his rostrum a man was haranguing the crowd. Mason and Mulroney joined the outer fringe of listeners without attracting any attention.

'That feller doing the talking is Joseph

Anton,' whispered Mulraney. 'I figure he's the big skookum he-wolf of the pack. Listen to him beller!'

Mason eyed the speaker with interest. Anton was a big man, not very tall, but with an enormous spread of shoulders and a barrel chest. He wore a forked beard that was black as bitumen and rippled down over his breast. His eyes were black and like smouldering windows of a burning house. His voice was peculiarly deep and resonant.

'Labour is the creator of all wealth, and wealth belongs to the creator. The wage system must be abolished. You, the creators, must do battle against those who are your self-imposed masters and crush them. You produce. The masters seize the rightful reward of your labour which should be yours and spend it on luxuries, dropping you but a crumb from the table. You are slaves, because you submit like slaves.'

Cheers interrupted him. He waited until the noise had subsided.

'There can be no compromise!' he bellowed. 'There can be no truce, no peace until the parasites who suck your blood are exterminated. The 'tools'—the ships, the factories—rightly belong to the workers who produce them. The tools must be surrendered to the workers, be surrendered or destroyed.'

Anton paused to take a drink of water. Mason's lips pursed in a soundless whistle.

119

'Whe-ew!' he breathed to his companion. 'Syndicalism at its worst! Comes close to being violent anarchism.'

'It's just so much sheep dip, but a lot of those scuts will swallow it,' Mulraney answered, 'and scare others into going along with them. You watch and see. Boss, there's going to be trouble.' Mason nodded.

'The unions!' roared Anton. Mason leaned forward tensely.

'The unions!' Anton repeated scornfully. 'Have they aided you? No! And why not? I will tell you why—because they are the servile instruments of the masters. They say the masters have rights, bargain with them. Bargain! No! There will be no bargaining. There will be war!'

Anton bowed his big head for a moment and stepped from the platform to be engulfed by the cheering crowd.

'Just as I thought, it is no bid to organize,' Mason said to his companion. 'The plan is to provoke a strike with violence, with whoever is back of this all set to take over the waterfront when the time is ripe. You're right, Terry, there's going to be trouble.'

'We'll give 'em trouble if they come foolin' around our end of the docks,' growled Mulraney. 'Now what?'

'Don't lose sight of Anton,' Mason said. 'Let's see what he does next.'

They moved a little closer and watched.

Soon Anton disengaged himself from his admirers, waved his hand and walked swiftly along Seventeenth Street alone.

'Follow him,' Mason said. 'I want to find out where he's going and who he's going to meet. Come on.'

They followed, keeping some distance to the rear.

Anton turned into Broadway and walked west. At Centre Street he turned again. His two shadows closed the gap a bit. Finally he paused in front of a saloon, then entered. It was the Crystal Bar.

Mason halted. 'I don't want to go in there, Terry,' he said. 'They know me there and I'd be spotted first off. I'll wait here at the corner. You go in and keep an eye on him. This is getting interesting.'

Mulraney entered the saloon. Mason loitered on the corner, smoking a cigarette. Some little time passed and Mulraney came out. Mason moved to join him.

'Well?' he asked.

'Well, he went right to Sam Gulden, who owns the joint, and they had a drink together and talked. After a bit they went into the back room together. A little later that cross-eyed bartender they call Long Tommy went in, too, and closed the door. I waited a while, but they didn't come out.'

'I see,' Mason said, and his eyes were like splinters of sapphire in his bronzed face. 'I should have known it. Terry, this is getting darned interesting. Let's go back to the waterfront and have a drink.'

Mason was silent during the walk back to Water Street, trying to evaluate what he had learned. They entered a bar frequented by the men of Bixby's gang and ordered drinks. Mason regarded his companion over the rim of his glass.

'Terry, what do you know about Anton, other than his name?' he asked.

'That's about all,' Mulraney replied. 'He showed up here out of nowhere a week or so back and started holding meetings. A talker, all right, ain't he?'

'He is,' Mason agreed. 'The sort to sway an ignorant crowd and incite to most anything.'

'Why did Anton go to see Sam Gulden?' Mulraney wondered.

'Because, unless I'm greatly mistaken, Sam Gulden and Long Tommy Hordle are back of this business,' Mason replied. 'They plan to take over the waterfront, and if we don't watch out they'll do just that.'

'Well, I'll be damned!' muttered Mulraney. Mason fell silent. Mulraney watched him respectfully.

The picture was gradually becoming clear to Mason's eyes. Shipping was Galveston's life blood, and whoever controlled the waterfront could just about dictate his own terms. That was why Honest John, Chauncey Weed and their associates at the Hall were concerned when it appeared that he, Mason, was gaining control until their fears were allayed by his attitude. Mason knew he still had influence along the docks, but he did not believe it strong enough to control the workers inflamed by the explosive exhortations of Joseph Anton and his ilk. He believed he could hold his own men in line, but they were in a minority and could not hope to make much headway against a general strike, if one were called.

He pondered the coincidence of the trouble starting the day after he arrived at Corpus Christi, and very quickly concluded it was no coincidence. Presumably the two killers who attempted to drown him had reported their mission successful. Gulden and Long Tommy Hordle, with the man they feared as an obstacle eliminated, or so they thought, had immediately swung into action. That mistake might well prove the foundation of sand that would bring their whole house of cards tumbling down.

'Tomorrow I'm going to the Hall and have a little talk with the folks there,' he told Mulroney. 'Let's go to bed.'

To make sure of his position before visiting the Hall, Mason first contacted the various contractors along the docks. He found them bewildered, apprehensive and bracing themselves for trouble. From all he got the same story: the men were sullen, mutinous and not working well, but so far there had been no demands for higher wages or shorter hours.

'They just seem on the prod against everybody and everything,' one told him. 'That darn Anton! Somebody ought to string him up to a light pole. He's the hellion most responsible for this. He's got the dockers hypnotized.'

Leaving the contractor still fulminating against Anton, Mason went to the Hall.

'Yes, we've been hearing about it,' said Chauncey Weed. 'Seems to be considerable unrest down there, but if there's a strike, we figure the shippers and the men will soon get together.'

'You figure wrong,' Mason said shortly. 'There'll be a strike, all right, with demands that can't possibly be met. Yes, there'll be a strike, and if something isn't done to prevent it, it'll be a strike with violence and destruction of property.'

'We can meet violence with violence, if necessary,' Weed replied.

'And that's just what I don't want to have happen,' Mason told him. 'Those fellows down there are dupes, uncomprehending pawns in an off-colour game. I don't want any of them hurt. Send in your police and special deputies and somebody will be hurt, which will be playing right into the hands of the devils who are back of this. They want people to get hurt, tempers inflamed, the longshoremen believing

124

that they have a real grievance with what's being done to them to prove it. They don't want a compromise and will make sure that one is impossible. Then, when they figure things have gone far enough, they'll bring in their own men, break the strike and take over. Then, very quickly, you'll have real trouble on your hands.'

'What the devil's to be done?' asked Honest John, genuinely alarmed at last.

'For the present, just sit tight,' Mason said. 'There's one flaw in their plan, a flaw they didn't anticipate, thinking it had been provided against.'

'What's that?' asked Weed.

'The loyalty of my men to myself and Jeth Bixby,' Mason replied. 'That may end giving them their come-uppance. I think it will, in one way or another. If they call the strike and my men refuse to go out, they'll feel forced to take action against them. That, I believe, will give us our chance to get the upper hand.'

'I don't see how any good can come from a pitched battle between two factions,' grumbled Honest John.

Mason chuckled. 'Out on the rangeland,' he replied, 'we sometimes lick a bad grass fire by building a back-fire against it. A practical application of the old adage, 'fighting fire with fire.' Maybe it'll work here.'

'Maybe,' conceded Honest John, 'but I'll have to see it to believe it.'

CHAPTER FIFTEEN

Three days later the strike was called, after demands utterly out of reason. The contractors and shippers couldn't meet them and said so in no uncertain terms. Joseph Anton, spokesman for the strikers, declared just as certainly that they could, and that until they were met, no cargo would move in or out of the port.

The strikers, however, could not present a solid front. Despite threats and exhortations, Jeth Bixby's crew kept right on working.

'And if the hellions come looking for trouble, they'll get it,' promised big Terence Mulraney. His mates stood ready to back him up.

'At night stay at this end of the docks and stick together,' Mason told the men. 'I don't think there will be any isolated cases of violence against you as that would not serve their purpose, but don't take chances.'

Mason slept very little during the days and nights that followed. He was confident that soon real trouble would break and didn't propose to be caught by surprise. The men were also constantly on the alert, and he felt confident that he would be forewarned of any serious development. Honest John, Chauncey Weed and their associates at the Hall had promised to back him up in any action he might see fit to take and he knew they would be good as their word. No extra police were sent to the waterfront, the authorities having agreed on a policy of watchful waiting.

'So long as there is no trouble, we won't do anything that might tend to incite it,' said Honest John. 'Mason says to sit tight and await developments. I think he's got the right idea.'

But Honest John and Mason both knew that it was only a matter of time till trouble would break. The strikers, prodded by the agitators, were getting in a dangerous mood, and the focus of wrath was the Bixby workers who refused to go out. Mason was not particularly surprised when Terence Mulraney, who had been scouting around, came to him with a grave face.

'It looks like showdown,' said Mulraney. 'Tomorrow afternoon they aim to march against us. They say they're going to run us all into the water.'

'Are they?' replied Mason. 'We'll see about that. Perhaps a little water would cool them down a bit. See you later, Terry; I'm heading for the Hall.'

At the Hall Mason outlined the plan he had evolved. His hearers listened in silence until he had finished, then grins split their countenances.

'Darned if I don't believe it will work,' chuckled Chauncey Weed. 'As Mason says, there is no blast so powerful, so withering as the blast of ridicule. Make a man look ridiculous and he loses force. Also, he's very likely to lose his sense of proportion and do something that will make him look even more ridiculous. That applies to a bunch of men as well as to an individual. Yes, I believe it'll work. If you gentlemen have no objection, I'm going to get in touch with the fire chief right away.'

Water Street was strangely deserted by noon the following day. Everybody knew that trouble was about to break and with it violence. The Bixby men, although greatly outnumbered, were fighters and would not readily submit to being shoved around. Sober people kept away from the waterfront streets. Most shopkeepers closed their doors.

'Where are the police?' was asked in many quarters. 'Why aren't they down here to bust it up before it starts?'

Shortly after noon the whole Bixby force of longshoremen left the docks and congregated near the west end of Water Street, lounging in the shadow of the low flat-roofed buildings that housed saloons and shops. Blaine Mason stood a little to the front, gazing down the street.

'Here they come, the sidewinders!' somebody shouted. 'Get set, boys, we'll give 'em hell.'

Far down the street a dense body of men

had streamed into view. They strode forward purposely, talking and shouting. Yells and cat calls went up as they sighted the Bixby men; their pace quickened. The Bixby men stiffened, eager for the battle even with the odds against them. Mason stood motionless, saying no word.

Nearer and nearer drew the mob of hooting strikers. In the forefront loomed Joseph Anton, his face alight with fanatical fire. Now they were close, brandishing clubs and baling hooks, yelping curses.

Mason took a long stride forward, and another, and halted. His voice rang out:

'That will be far enough. Any farther and you'll be sorry.'

The words and his appearance gave the strikers pause. They knew Blaine Mason and respected his ability.

'What's he got up his sleeve?' ran the mutter along the front ranks. 'Look out! He's bad!'

The march had almost come to a standstill when Joseph Anton's mighty bellow drowned all other sounds.

'To hell with him! Come on!'

The strikers surged forward. Mason raised his hand.

From the open windows of the buildings lining the street and over the false fronts burst streams of icy water driven with terrific force. They moved down the front ranks. The sound of the impact was like the tearing of heavy sail-cloth. Men knocked to the ground tried to rise and were knocked down again. Some of the nozzles raised a little and bowled over those behind, driving them like flies down the street. More and more streams joined the deluge. From the alley behind the buildings came the sound of pumpers working at full speed.

Drenched, blinded, bruised and strangled, the strikers broke and fled this way and that like whipped and soused puppies. From the Bixby men came a roar of laughter. It was echoed by groups of people watching from a safe distance till it seemed the whole waterfront was a-bellow with mirth.

Blaine Mason raised his hand again. Instantly the jets of water were shut off. But not the laughter. It continued, loud and long.

From the scattered ranks of the demoralized strikers burst a huge figure roaring curses. His eyes blazing with a madman's rage, Joseph Anton charged straight for Blaine Mason who braced himself to receive the onslaught.

The Bixby men surged forward, but Mason shouted warningly, 'Stand back! This is my game.'

Huge fists flailing, Anton rushed. Mason weaved aside and hit him, left and right. The blows staggered him but did not stop him. He surged forward and his counters, which he could not avoid, staggered Mason in turn. He hit out with both hands, connected, and received solid blows in return. Blood streamed down his face from a cut over one eye.

Mason knew he had a fight on his hands. Anton was an even heavier man than Kearns, and he was quicker. He forced Mason to give ground, then was brought up himself by a straight right that sent blood flying from his nose and mouth. Back he came, pounding Mason's body with left hooks that had force behind them.

Mason fought desperately now, savagely, taking advantage of every opening. Anton was a madman with the strength of a madman and seemed insensible to punishment.

His fighting stance was peculiar, his great shoulders stooping forward, his left arm drawn back, his right flung across his chest. Most of his blows were struck with his left, but Mason watched that great right fist and knotted forearm, for it was in that passive right that he believed his danger really lay.

He was able to block most of Anton's blows, but when one landed squarely it jarred him from head to foot. His forearms were bruised to the elbow, his knuckles split and bleeding, his breath came in gasps, and always he watched that deadly right with which Anton struck so seldom.

Presently it came, the blow Anton had been husbanding his strength to give, with arm and shoulder and body behind it—quick as a flash, resistless as a cannonball.

But Mason was ready. He leaped sideways, and as he leaped he struck clean and true upon the angle of the jaw. Anton spun around and fell and lay with arms wide stretched. Mason stood watching him, breathing in great gulps.

Slowly Anton got to his hands and knees, hung motionless for a moment in his grotesque crouch like a stricken ape, gathering his strength. Then he surged erect and faced Mason. His right hand streaked to his left armpit. Mason's right shoulder hunched a little. The two guns boomed almost as one.

Almost but not quite. Mason's Colt wisped smoke a split second before Anton pulled trigger.

Anton screamed hoarsely. He reeled back, fell to the ground and rolled over and over, clutching his bullet-smashed hand from which blood spurted. His gun, one butt plate knocked off, clattered across the cobbles almost to the feet of the rigid strikers.

'Don't touch it!' Mason warned, his Colt jutting forward. Those closest to the fallen arm drew back as from a deadly snake.

Mason strode to Anton, seized him by the collar and jerked him to his feet.

'Get going,' he told him. 'You're not hurt as bad as you think you are. Get going, I say. Go to the two skunks who sent you here and tell them their little scheme didn't work. And, Anton, don't come back. If you do I'll kill you.

Get going!'

Groaning and cursing, Anton lurched off. Mason watched him round a corner, then turned to the demoralized strikers.

'Well,' he said, 'don't you think it's about time you fellows stopped acting the fool?'

Nobody answered him. The strikers seemed bereft of speech. They glanced sheepishly at each other.

Mason drew a roll of bills from his pocket. He stepped forward, handed the money to a man in the front rank who took it mechanically.

'There's a hundred dollars,' he said. 'Enough to buy beer for everybody. I hope I'll see you all back to work in the morning.'

The strikers goggled at him, then gave a ragged cheer and hurried after the man with the money who was heading for the nearest saloon.

Mason turned to his own men. 'All right, boys,' he said, 'let's get back to work. And at quitting time line up at the office for an extra day's pay with which to celebrate.'

There was another cheer. The longshoremen, laughing and chattering, trooped off to work.

Chauncey Weed, nonchalant, assured, appeared from a nearby saloon and sauntered forward.

'Mason,' he said, 'I sure wouldn't want you for an enemy. Or for a rival, either,' he added whimsically and passed on.

Mason gazed after him. 'You don't need to bother on that score,' he apostrophized the departing Weed. 'I was removed from that category long ago.'

In the office Mason doctored his injuries which were not serious. The chore finished, he sat down, rolled a cigarette and addressed Jeth Bixby.

'Well, that little matter is attended to, and I don't think we'll have any more trouble from the boys,' he said. 'I wonder what will bust loose next.'

Meanwhile, in the back room of the Crystal Bar, Sam Gulden and Long Tommy were having a highly unpleasant interview with Joseph Anton, the agitator. Anton, his right hand swathed in blood-stained bandages, his face contorted with anger, shook his one good fist in Gulden's face.

'You told me that big ice-eyed hellion would be kept away from here,' he bawled accusingly. 'And what happens? I find him right here bucking me, with the cards stacked against me. Of all the bungling, horned toads, you two are the limit!'

'We thought we had him kept away definitely,' defended Long Tommy. 'We certainly got word to that effect. Either somebody plain lied or something slipped somewhere, I don't know which. I wish I did know for sure, then there'd be one double-crosser less. And why the devil did you have to tackle him? I told you he was bad. He thrashed the toughest man on the waterfront when he came here, and he's been raising Cain ever since. Why did you jump him?'

'Because I lost my head,' Anton admitted frankly. 'But you catch a stream of ice water at sixty pounds pressure in the face and see how you like it.'

'And after he'd walloped you, you had to try and pull on him,' broke in Gulden. 'I don't believe there's a faster man on the draw in this end of Texas. It's a wonder he didn't kill you. I reckon he figured you weren't worth killing and just shot your iron out of your hand instead of drilling you dead centre.'

'All right, all right,' growled Anton, 'I took a licking from a better man, two ways, that's all. I'm not complaining about that. What's got me riled is the fact you two fell down on your end of the job and let me in for what happened. Well, that's one of the hazards of my business, having to deal with incompetents. We'll settle our score and then I'm leaving this infernal town. Wish I'd never seen it. Here's the account—come across.'

After Anton had departed, mumbling curses, a fat fee in his pocket, Gulden and Long Tommy looked at each other blankly.

'Well, now what?' asked the former.

'I guess there's only one thing to do,' Long Tommy said slowly. 'Do as Anton did, admit

135

we're licked and lay off Mason. You can't kill him and you can't outsmart him. He's given us our come-uppance at every turn. I wish you hadn't monkeyed with him in the first place.'

'It was your notion,' snarled Gulden.

'You're a liar,' Long Tommy said dispassionately.

'Well, anyhow, you put the idea in my head,' said Gulden.

'I merely mentioned he was packing a lot of dinero,' countered Long Tommy. 'It was you who decided to try and tie on to it. Well, you tied on to it, and got a grizzly bear by the tail at the same time. What we've got to figure is how to let go with as few bites and scratches as possible. By the way, I suppose you've still got his forty-thousand pesos in the safe, or have you?'

Gulden glared at him. 'Lock that door,' he said. Long Tommy did so. Gulden went to a big safe in a corner of the room and twirled the combination knob. Swinging the safe door open, he drew out a stout canvas sack and dumped several packets of bills of large denomination on the table.

'There it is, divided up. Count it if you want to,' he spat at his partner. 'I'm keeping it in the safe against an emergency. And if things keep on going as they have been of late, there'll be an emergency of one sort or another, and soon. Business has fallen off to nothing. The cowhands don't come in here any more, nor the longshoremen. And those double-crossers at the Hall make a point of staying away. Mason seems to have them hypnotized. How does he do it?'

'I'll tell you how,' said Long Tommy. 'It's because he's what you and I never were and never will be—a squareshooter. People trust him.'

'You may have something there,' Gulden conceded heavily. 'Funny, ain't it, Tom. You start cutting corners and keep on cutting them closer and closer until—'

'Until you end up cutting your own throat,' Long Tommy interrupted with a sardonic grin.

The following morning found the strikers back at work, cheerful and content. And there was no doubt in anybody's mind as to who was the Boss of the Waterfront!

CHAPTER SIXTEEN

Blaine mason felt that he should be in a complacent and satisfied mood. The phony strike had been successfully broken by a few lengths of fire hose and a few pumpers. Nobody had been hurt, with resulting bitterness, except Anton, the professional agitator, who had it coming. Gulden and Hordle's attempt to take over the waterfront was frustrated, and he himself enjoyed a position of strengthened authority. He had definitely thwarted Hordle's political ambitions and was well on the way to ruining Gulden financially. His campaign of vengeance was nearing a successful consummation. Yes, he ought to feel fine, but he didn't. He was gloomy and depressed. Leaving the office, he walked slowly along the docks in the golden sunshine. Men waved their hands and shouted greetings which he automatically answered in kind. He had come a long way in less than two years, he reflected. Why should he not rejoice? Why should he not be filled with pride in his achievements? Instead they seemed but hollow mockeries that jeered at his discontent.

Mason sighed deeply and gazed with unseeing eyes at the glory of the day.

The reason for it all? A woman!

At the far end of the docks, Mason turned and slowly retraced his steps. There was work to do, and in work one can forget sometimes.

When he reached the office a surprise awaited him. Engaged in animated conversation with Jeth Bixby were old Judson Walters and his daughter Cora. Mason was glad to see them both and said so. Cora gazed at his bruised face.

'You've been fighting,' she said accusingly.

'Sort of,' Mason admitted with a grin.

'I was telling them about what happened,' broke in Bixby. 'I hadn't got to the fight yet. Now as I was saying—'

Mason sat down, rolled a cigarette and resigned himself to listen. There was no stopping Jeth once he got started. His two listeners appeared deeply absorbed in his graphic account.

When he had finished, Cora's eyes registered distinct approval as they rested on Mason. Old Judson's became voluble.

'Son, you're all right,' he chuckled. 'You handled that one like a master. Wish I'd been a day earlier to see it. Klingman is bringing the boat back tonight after the performance, and we figured to be here for the first show which he says will go on tomorrow night. Mind showing us around a bit? This section looks interesting.'

His guests appeared to thoroughly enjoy their tour of the waterfront. So did Mason, and as Cora accorded him a flattering attention, his spirits rose. Perhaps things weren't so bad they couldn't be mended. She was a beauty, all right; intelligent, charming, also, with a vivid sense of humour. By the time he escorted her and her father to their hotel, he was feeling a good sight better. He looked forward to the coming evening, having promised to take them to the night spot favoured by Chauncey Weed and his associates of the Hall.

The big restaurant and bar were crowded with mostly men when Mason entered with Cora on his arm. Conversation stilled, heads turned, eyes shone with frank admiration.

'Good Lord!' exclaimed Honest John. 'Ain't that just about the finest looking couple you ever laid eyes on! That's Judson Walters' gal. Takes after her mother. I've known Judson for a long time. Fine old feller. That jigger Mason sure does get around. Mighty pretty gal, don't you think, Chaunce?'

'Why—why yes, she is,' Chauncey agreed lamely. 'Yes, she is.'

After his guests were seated, Mason strolled to the bar to greet his acquaintances there. After a few minutes of general conversation Mason said, 'Come over and meet my friends, Chauncey. John, I believe you know Mr. Walters. I'll bring him here after we eat.'

Weed followed Mason to the table. He looked slightly dazed. His face was flushed, his hands nervous, both conditions out of keeping with the usually suave and collected Mr. Weed. When Mason introduced him, he mumbled something almost incoherent, took the hand Cora extended, and forgot to bow. Miss Walters' eyes were unusually bright, and the colour in her cheeks had deepened.

Weed accepted an invitation to dine with them. Shortly he recovered his aplomb and conversed easily. After the meal, which took quite a while, Mason suggested to Walters that they go to the bar and visit with the boys.

'I'm sure Cora and Mr. Weed will excuse us for a little while,' he said. 'John and the others wish to talk with Mr. Walters.'

'Why, yes, yes, certainly, of course,' Mr. Weed said absently. Cora nodded her shapely head and smiled.

At the bar Walters and the other oldtimers there finally drifted into reminiscence. Mason listened for a while, then turned back to the table. He took a few steps and paused.

Cora and Chauncey Weed were holding hands above the table and looking into one anther's eyes in a way that was not to be misinterpreted.

Blaine Mason abruptly experienced a great sorrow for Sharon Grant. For a moment he gazed at the engrossed pair. Then he turned and went out alone.

The Island Queen steamed into the harbour the following afternoon. Once again the tugs tooted, the foghorns blared. The Queen had been accepted as a Galveston institution and was greeted accordingly.

'Sure was a fine trip, and a paying one,' Caleb Klingman told Mason. 'Yep, we made a hit at Corpus Christi. It was Mayor Arbuckle himself who persuaded us to stay the extra week. He sure thinks well of you, too. Sent regards and said he hopes to see you soon.'

It was with some trepidation that Mason mounted the gangplank that evening in company of the Walters, father and daughter, and Chauncey Weed. Sharon and Dud Gavens awaited them at the entrance to the

141

auditorium.

If Sharon harboured any resentment at seeing Weed consorting with Cora Walters, she didn't show it. The two girls greeted each other effusively and moved away together. Gavens proceeded to give a graphic account of the stay at Corpus Christi.

'Guess we'll have to take her to Port Isabel and Brownsville, too,' he concluded. 'They sent word they'd like to have us over there.'

'That's a notion, all right,' Mason agreed. 'We'll do it after the stay here.'

In the course of the evening's performance, Mason thought Sharon had never before danced so well or sung so sweetly. She was gay, animated, her eyes glowing with what looked to be a light of happiness. Mason couldn't understand it. But then she was an actress and accustomed to donning whatever expression suited the moment. He wondered morosely if there were tears beneath the laughter. He met her after the show was over and they stood by the rail together. Cora and Chauncey Weed were also standing by the rail, some distance away, absorbed in one another.

'Looks like they're both plumb smitten,' Mason was forced to say.

'Yes, doesn't it,' agreed Sharon. 'They make a wonderful couple—just suited for each other.'

'You don't mind?' he asked hesitantly.

'Mind? Why should I? They're both my

friends and I'm glad to see them happy.'

'But I thought you and Chauncey were interested in each other,' he stammered.

'Oh, Mr. Weed is interested in me, all right,' Sharon returned cheerfully. 'He has a keen nose for business. He believes, although quite probably he's wrong, that I would be a big attraction at his dinner place in Houston, which would mean money in his pocket.'

Mason looked and felt dazed. 'And you're not interested in him?' he hesitated.

Sharon turned to face him, and her eyes were brimming with laughter.

'Blaine,' she said, 'sometimes I forget that you're a wise, successful man, and I think you're just a silly goose.'

Mason stared in bewilderment. 'Shay, what the devil do you mean by that?' he asked. Belatedly it came to him that it seemed he was always asking her what she meant by this, that, or the other.

'You'll find out some day, I hope,' she replied.

Cora and Weed moved over to join them, and a conversation that was threatening to become interesting came to an end.

Judson Walters and his daughter remained in Galveston two more days. Sharon and Mason and Chauncey Weed saw them off on the train.

'Don't forget to tell them, dear,' Cora called from the rear platform as the train pulled out.

Sharon and Mason turned expectantly to Weed. Both had a pretty good notion as to what was coming.

'We're going to be married on the eleventh at the ranchhouse,' Weed said, flushing a little. 'Mr. Walters wants time to get all his friends together for the wedding. And we hope that you, Sharon, will be maid of honour, and Blaine the best man.'

'Of course we will!' Mason instantly accepted for both of them. 'And congratulations, Chauncey! She's a wonderful girl!'

'And you, Mr. Weed,' said Sharon, 'are a man who knows his own mind, which is something.'

This time Mason didn't ask her what the devil she meant, but he wondered.

Mason saw little of Sharon in the next few days that followed. The harbour was crowded with shipping and the longshoremen worked day and night to relieve the congestion. Mason, with a thousand things to attend to, hardly had time to eat and grab an occasional hour of sleep.

Finally things eased up a bit. Mason, thoroughly worn out, went to bed shortly after dark and slept until late morning. He awoke with a feeling of oppression. His room, usually comfortably cool, was hot. The air was heavy and sultry. It was a chore to bathe and shave and dress.

144

'Storm coming, sure as the devil,' he muttered. He hoped it wouldn't last long, for in a couple of days he and Sharon would catch a train for Bay City and the Bradded L ranch. Wiping away the sweat that beaded his face, he headed for the street and some breakfast.

It was one of the Gulf's yellow mornings when it shows itself in its somberest, most baleful mood. The sky was smouldering ochre. The waves were tipped with a hot bronze that curdled to amber in the hollows. The long, narrow dark green leaves of the oleanders for which Galveston was famous hung dispiritedly in the still air; their large red, white and purple double flowers seemed filmed with a phosphorescent lemon. The sulphur-stained buildings of the waterfront glowed dully saffron. And the heat pressed down like a steam-charged blanket.

Mason ate listlessly although he was hungry. Raising food to his lips was an effort. Every movement was an effort, in fact. After smoking a couple of tasteless cigarettes, he repaired to Bixby's office. On the wall hung a thermometer and a barometer. The temperature was 91. He glanced at the barometer and whistled. It stood at 29.50, the lowest Mason could recall seeing. For these latitudes 30.15 was about normal. He tapped the instrument lightly; it responded obligingly by dropping to 29.45. Mason whistled again.

Entering the office, he found Bixby

swearing and mopping his face.

'Hellish weather,' he growled.

'It is,' Mason agreed. He glanced over some reports, abruptly left the office and mingled with the longshoremen going about their tasks.

'Take it easy,' he cautioned. 'The work needs to be done, but don't over-exert yourselves. You can get a heat stroke easily in this weather. If you feel your skin getting dry, knock off and head for the shade. I'll have hot coffee handy. Drink it, and don't go into the sun again till your skin is moist.'

'Over toward the other end they're driving the men, trying to get those British freighters loaded in case of a storm,' observed Mulraney.

'They're crazy,' Mason said. 'I'll go over there and say a few words to them. Human lives are more important than freight arriving at its destination on schedule.' He proceeded to do so and got results. Since the strike and the part he played in it, nobody on the waterfront argued with Blaine Mason.

He surveyed the channel which was a sheet of molten brass. Making his way slowly to the Gulf shore he stood gazing into the southeast. Although there was not a breath of air stirring, there was a surprisingly heavy surf along the beach. Mason shook his head as he regarded the huge swell that had set in.

'And it's coming straight from the southeast,' he muttered. 'Coming from open water stretching to the Caribbean. I don't like it.'

He returned to the office, still walking slowly. The heat was even more intense, the air heavier; he experienced a slight difficulty in breathing if he quickened his pace even a little. He paused at the Hall for a short talk with Chauncey Weed and to ask a favour.

'So you think there's a storm coming?' asked Weed.

'There is,' Mason replied.

'Guess it won't amount to much,' Weed said cheerfully.

'Perhaps not,' Mason replied, 'but I'm not so sure,' he added, thinking of that ominously low barometer.

'Okay,' said Weed, 'we'll take care of the stuff for you. The old Hall can take it, no matter how rough it gets, I think.'

A wind was blowing from the northwest when Mason left the Hall. Ragged streamers of cloud were hurrying across the yellow sky. At the office he had a lot of paper work to do and got busy without delay. It was full dark, hot and sultry, when he arose and looked out of the door.

'Guess we'll have a storm, all right,' said Bixby. 'But it won't amount to much, coming from the northwest.'

'But you'll notice that the wind is veering around. It's coming from the west now, by slightly south.'

Mason went out for a look at the barometer.

He struck a light and peered at the instrument, staring unbelievingly while the match flickered in his fingers. The thing stood fully an inch lower than the last time he looked at it. He re-entered the office, sat down and wrote a few sentences on a sheet of paper which he folded and thrust in his pocket.

'I'll be back in a little while,' he told Bixby who was preparing to go. 'Leave a light burning.' He hurried to the Island Queen and searched out Captain Pete Blake.

'Pete,' he said, 'get steam up as quickly as you can. Head for Corpus Christi as fast as your engines will get you there. Over there I think you'll miss the brunt of the storm and should be able to ride it out. As soon as you get there, hunt up Mayor Arbuckle and give him this note. He's my friend and will work with you. Load the Queen with blankets, clothing, food and medicine. Plenty of bandages. As soon as the storm lets up, head back here as fast as you can. What you'll pack is going to be needed badly.'

The captain stared. 'You think we're in for a really bad blow?' he asked.

'We're in for such a blow as this island has never known in recorded history,' Mason replied. 'The one that wrecked the Red House in Jean Lafitte's day and killed dozens of people was a zephyr compared to what this one is going to be. The sea is liable to sweep this island clean. At the very least there will be terrible damage and, I fear, loss of life. The wind is veering to the southeast. This thing is headed straight for Galveston Island over a thousand miles of open water.'

'Blaine, I've a notion you're taking it too seriously,' said Blake. 'We've had blows here before and always managed to weather them.'

'Pete,' Mason said, 'the barometer is standing at 28.45. That's just about the end of the world in these latitudes. And it's still falling.'

It was Blake's turn to whistle. 'I hadn't noticed,' he confessed. 'We had a little card game in the cabin and I didn't pay much attention to the weather.'

'Pay attention to it now,' Mason said tersely. 'Get going!' He turned as Blake hurried away to find Sharon Grant at his elbow.

'You're staying, Blaine?' she asked.

'Of course,' he replied. 'Take care of yourself, Shay.'

'I will,' she promised. She turned and hurried to her cabin.

Mason went ashore, hunted up Terry Mulraney and several other huskies and gave them some instructions.

'I'll be ready for you in about an hour,' he concluded. As he finished speaking he heard the pound of the Island Queen's engines; she was under way. He watched her lights dim into the distance and headed for the office. The wind had veered a bit more and was now blowing from almost due south, as he could tell by the heat of it on his face. It was not refreshing, being hot and muggy, a slow, steady wind that pressed against his body like water.

A light burned in the office. Mason entered and paused in astonishment. Seated in Bixby's chair was a small figure, shapely legs comfortably crossed.

'Shay!' he exclaimed. 'What the devil are you doing here?'

'Waiting for you,' Sharon replied composedly.

'But—but,' he sputtered, 'you should be on the boat. All hell's liable to break loose here before another twenty-four hours have passed.'

'Let it break,' she returned. Mason muttered an exasperated oath.

'I figured you'd be on the boat, and safe,' he growled. 'You shouldn't be here. Why—'

'You're here, aren't you?' she interrupted.

'Yes, but—'

'And a woman who doesn't stay with her man when the going is rough isn't much of a woman,' she interrupted again.

'Her man!' he repeated dazedly.

'Of course. That's what you've been for quite a while, only I was beginning to wonder if you'd ever find it out.'

Mason stared. For the life of him he couldn't utter a word. Suddenly Sharon laughed, a merry, ringing laugh. She slipped from the chair, walked over to him and stood on tip-toe.

'Please bend your tall head, my dear,' she said. 'I want to pay you back the one you gave me that night in the moonlight.'

CHAPTER SEVENTEEN

Mechanically he obeyed. Her lips were warm, soft, dewy-fresh on his. Mason snapped out of his semi-trance. He crushed her to him, his arms about her like bands of steel. She gasped, but returned his kisses as fiercely as he gave them.

'Wasn't I the fool!' he said when they paused for breath.

'You were,' she agreed gaily, 'and I suppose you always will be, in one way or another. Perhaps that's why I love you. You're so refreshingly different, so free from conceit. Not that that doesn't grow bothersome after a while. A girl doesn't mind eating her heart out a little, but there's a limit.'

Mason laughed for pure joy. He lifted her from the floor, cradled her in his arms a moment, then gently deposited her in the chair.

'Stay there and look beautiful—you couldn't look any other way,' he said. 'I've got work to do, and time's getting short.'

He began stuffing documents into cases that stood ready to hand. 'I'm moving all the records to the Hall,' he explained. 'Weed will take care of them for me.'

'I'll help,' Sharon said. 'Hand me the papers and I'll pack them; a woman can always do a neater job.'

They had very nearly finished the chore when Terry Mulraney and half a dozen other longshoremen entered. They looked surprised, grinned and ducked their heads to Sharon.

'All set to go,' Mason told them. 'Terry, make sure Weed stores them on the second floor. The Hall is sturdily built and I think it can withstand any amount of wind, but water is something else again.'

'You figure we'll get water on the island?' Mulraney asked.

'I don't know,' Mason replied, 'but we may. The highest elevation is nowhere more than eight feet. Wouldn't take much of a rise to inundate that. We'll just have to wait and see.'

The men shouldered their burdens and trooped out. Mason turned to Sharon.

'What am I going to do with you?' he asked. 'Caleb Klingman can put you up for the night if you don't mind rather rough quarters. Otherwise I'll take you to an hotel.'

'I'm staying where you stay,' she declared flatly. 'And I expect I've slept in rougher quarters than Caleb will provide.'

'All right,' Mason agreed. 'We'll get

something to eat first.'

Outside the office, Sharon raised her head. 'Listen to that eerie moan,' she said. 'What is it, the wind?'

'It's the Gulf water worrying against the jetties,' Mason replied grimly. 'I've heard it before, during the storm last summer, but never so deep-toned.'

'It shudders the very air,' she said. 'Sounds like a great animal in pain.'

They ate at a waterfront restaurant favoured by shippers. Several men came over to talk with Mason. Their faces were grave.

'We'll batten down as best we can,' Mason told them. 'We may not catch it too bad over here, but I'm worried about the Gulf shore. The buildings there are flimsy, and a lot of people live in them. Of course, if there is a real tidal wave, as there could be, we may suffer a backwash that won't do us any good.'

'You figure it's going to be really bad?' one asked.

'I'm afraid we're in for a regular Caribbean-Gulf hurricane, and there's no worse anywhere in the world,' Mason replied. 'All indications point that way. Another eighteen hours or so should tell the story. It might veer and give us only the fringe of the storm. But the wind is blowing from almost due southeast now and that's bad. I'm afraid Galveston is going to be directly in its path. I'll be with you shortly.'

Caleb Klingman welcomed Sharon and

didn't appear unduly surprised. 'I've got a good little room almost across the hall from yours, Blaine,' he said. 'She ought to be comfortable there.'

'I'm sure I will,' Sharon replied. 'Yes, this will be fine,' she added as Caleb lit a lamp. 'And thank you so much.'

Mason deposited her small handbag in the room, picked her up and lifted her lightly to his lips.

'See you tomorrow, honey,' he promised.

She clung to him a moment. 'Be careful, dear,' she begged.

'Nothing to worry about tonight,' he replied cheerfully. 'This sort of thing doesn't come all of a sudden. It'll be a slow build-up. We're just going to try and get ready for it.'

With a nod and a smile, he departed. Sharon closed the door very softly.

Every longshoreman on the docks was pressed into service and they worked until far into the night. Buildings were sandbagged. Cables were stretched across the roofs of the less substantial structures and anchored to heavy stakes driven deep into the ground. All shipping was double-moored and every precaution taken against the crafts breaking adrift. Most of the ships had already hastily put out to sea, preferring to ride out the storm in open water.

Finally Mason called a halt. 'Get some rest,' he told the tired workers. 'We're liable to have our hands full tomorrow.'

The dockers trooped off, weary but cheerful. Some paused to look back at Mason standing tall and straight against a background of smoking flares.

'That jigger can swing a maul harder than any man I know,' one remarked to a companion.

'And he don't spare himself,' rejoined the other. 'Yep, he's a boss worth working for, is the Old Man.'

Mason walked slowly to the roominghouse, filled with foreboding. The wind was blowing straight from the southeast and growing noticeably stronger. The moan of the tortured jetties had risen to a thin whine that weaved through the deep-toned crashing of the breakers. Not a star was in sight. The sky was dead black, a shroud pressing down on the cowering earth. His hands were sore, his arms aching from exhausting labour, but despite his uneasiness, he was at peace as he had not been for a very long time.

As he climbed the stairs, he saw there was a streak of light seeping from under the door of his room. He opened it to find Sharon, in a silken robe that matched the colour of her eyes, curled up in a chair by the window.

'Shay, why aren't you asleep?' he scolded.

'I couldn't sleep till you came back,' she replied. 'So I came in here where I could watch the street. Now I can, maybe. Oh, for gracious sake! Put out that light! The window's wide open and it's too hot to draw the shade!'

When Mason awoke to the grey twilight of a sunless day, the wind was shaking the building. He dressed hurriedly and descended to the street where a wild scene met his eyes. Although it was full day, the sky was black, with rolling masses of clouds weaving into fantastic shapes. The force of the wind staggered him. He clutched the side of the house to regain his balance. Making his way along the street with difficulty, he entered a restaurant and ordered a bountiful breakfast, for the Lord alone knew when he would get a chance to eat again.

The place was crowded with apprehensive faces. Now there was no doubt but a regular rip-snorter of a hurricane was headed straight for Galveston Island. Already the wind was nearing hurricane force and the real storm was still far off. Mason congratulated himself on sending the Island Queen to Corpus Christi. He believed she would be safe there, and the cargo she would bring back might well be sorely needed.

Yes, it would be bad. But not even he conceived the horror Galveston would know before another day dawned. September eighth—Galveston's hideous day and night.

After making sure everything to safeguard the waterfront was being done, Mason walked across to the Gulf shore. It was all he could do to make his way windward against the mighty torrent of air. At the coast a scene of terror met his eyes. Through the clouds of spray, he had glimpses of long grey ridges running to an appalling height thundering in upon the beach far beyond high water mark. The ground shook to their frightful pounding. Dark ragged clouds scudded by so close overhead it seemed one could reach up and touch them. Farther to the southeast they were of a dull greenish-purple shading to grey where the rays of the sun struggled in vain to pierce the veil. The bellow of the wind dwarfed even the tremulous voice of the breakers.

Mason looked back. The island appeared so low, so pitiably insecure.

Everywhere men were working frantically to bulwark the frailer structures, like ants striving to repair the damage done by a heavy-treading foot. And futilely, Mason thought, as if the foot were returning to stamp once again.

He talked with several of the groups, advising them to evacuate the flimsy dwellings and seek refuge in the possibly safer centre of the town. But the people were stubborn and didn't want to abandon their homes, insisting they would be safe in them. Mason returned to Water Street, roused up Sharon and took her to the restaurant for breakfast.

'This is terrible!' she shrilled above the uproar as they staggered along the street. 'Will it get much worse, Blaine?'

'This is nothing,' he told her grimly. 'The wind has hardly reached hurricane force as yet. Before it's finished, it may attain a velocity nearly double what it is now.

'But I think our real danger is from the Gulf,' he added. 'Winds of a hundred miles an hour and more not only kick up huge waves, but there is a considerable rise in the level of the sea itself caused by the sharp drop in atmospheric pressure. But we'll weather it somehow; don't be afraid.'

She snuggled closer. 'With you I'll never be afraid,' she said softly. 'Only I want to be with you, no matter what happens. Promise me I will.'

'I promise,' he said. 'We'll see it out together.'

Before reaching the restaurant, Mason stopped at a sailors' outfitting store and bought heavy slickers for Sharon and himself, the shopkeeper fortunately having one very small size in stock.

'We'll need them,' Mason told her. 'The temperature's dropping, and we'll get rain any minute now. And when I say rain, I mean *rain*!'

Mason was right about the rain. They took their time at the table and when they left the eating house, the rain was driving in horizontal sheets before the wind. Blinded, deafened, they fought their way to the roominghouse. The little room on the second floor was warm and comfortable and the thick walls shut out

158

most of the tumult. They removed their streaming slickers and hung them to drip. Sharon slipped off her shoes and stockings and Mason dried her small but sturdy feet with a towel.

'I'm heading for the office to see how Jeth is making out, after I've had a cigarette with you,' Mason told her. 'No, I'm not going far away, and I'll keep you with me tonight, although I think you'd be safer here. This house is built of old ship's timbers and will withstand quite a battering.'

'If you don't take me with you tonight I'll come out looking for you,' she threatened. 'I mean it.'

Mason believed her. He donned his slicker, kissed her, and went out into the fury of the storm. He paused for a look at the barometer before entering the office and experienced something like a thrill of horror when he saw it stood at 28.01.

'We're going to get water. Sure as hell we're going to get water,' he muttered.

When he entered the office, closing the door behind him with difficulty, he found Jeth Bixby seated comfortably in his chair, smoking a cigar. He waved a greeting.

'Old shack's shaking a bit, but I've a notion she'll stand up,' he said. 'Think it'll get much worse?'

'It will,' Mason replied. 'The eye of the hurricane is still a long ways off. The full force

159

will strike here sometime during the night. I'm very greatly afraid many of the houses on the Gulf side won't stand it, and there's liable to be a loss of life if people insist on remaining there. If we get water, too, and I'm afraid we will, it will loosen the foundations and the wind will topple the shacks. At the very best, there are going to be a great many people homeless.'

Bixby regarded him a moment in silence. 'And suppose,' he said slowly, 'suppose the sea really rises and sweeps the island?'

'Jeth,' Mason replied, 'I'm trying not to think of that.'

'Then you believe that is just what is going to happen?'

'I'm afraid so,' Mason replied in a tired voice. 'Nobody seems willing to agree with me. That's why I tried to persuade people on the Gulf side to abandon their homes and come to the centre of the town where the solidly constructed buildings will provide something like shelter. The unbelievably low barometer reading causes me to fear that's just what's going to happen. So much so that I'm going to the Hall and see if I can get somebody there to do something about it.'

With difficulty Mason fought his way through the streaming, deserted streets to the Hall. He found Chauncey Weed there and laid the case before him. Weed listened politely enough, but Mason could see that in his mind he tended to minimize the danger.

'I'll try and get the council together—most of the boys are at home—and see what they have to say,' he promised at length. Mason went back to Water Street, barely able to make headway against the rain and the wind which was now blowing at true hurricane force. Time and again he was forced to dodge bits of flying debris, some of it not small.

Chauncey Weed was good as his word. By heroic efforts he managed to get together a quorum of the council. But it took time, and more precious time was lost in argument and debate. When a decision was finally reached, it was too late.

By late afternoon the wind had attained a velocity of more than a hundred miles an hour. The rain no longer merely descended. It was driven on the wings of the wind in horizontal cataracts that stung the flesh like shot, even under clothing. Roofs were blown off. Poorly constructed buildings were flattened. A ship snapped its mooring and crashed into two others. One was sunk. The two remaining afloat were finally anchored and secured after frenzied efforts on the part of the sailors and longshoremen.

The lower parts of the city along the Gulf and elsewhere were inundated. And at tardy last the people of Galveston were fully awake to their danger. Some fled to the mainland, but before night that avenue of escape was closed. Others crowded into the central part of the town or on to other spots of higher elevation in an often vain effort to escape the wrath of the storm.

Night fell, a night of utter darkness filled with the ravings of the wind, the dashing of the rain and the roar of the sea. But piercing the frightful tumult was a still more terrible sound, the screams and cries of agony and terror.

Most people who had homes still standing remained in them, fearful of the dangers of flying debris and rushing water. But some dared the fury of the elements to carry on the work of mercy and rescue. Among these were Blaine Mason, with Sharon Grant clinging to his side, and Chauncey Weed. They toiled in the bleak terrain between Thirty-ninth and Fifty-third Streets, leading frightened, bewildered people to the safety of newly completed Fort Crocket, binding wounds, splinting broken limbs.

Mason, lined and haggard himself, his hands torn and bleeding, watched Sharon anxiously. Her face was pinched and white, her lips ash-grey, but her blue eyes blazed with fierce courage and determination and she steadfastly refused to seek shelter or rest. The formerly debonaire Chauncey Weed was a wooden-featured automaton, performing tasks beyond his strength without complaint.

Once Mason was nearly drowned as he burrowed beneath the wreckage of a fallen house, waves smoking about and over him, to rescue a child pinned there. But he made it out, strangling and retching, with the child only slightly injured.

The night of horror wore slowly on. The wind screamed, the rain fell. The tormented waters roared and bellowed. Fiery fingers of lightning weaved across the black sky. The thunder rolled but was scarcely heard above the tumult below. Mason and his companions made trip after trip to the fort, bearing with them the injured they rescued from collapsed buildings. All three were on the verge of prostration from fatigue, but they grimly carried on.

Finally the rain ceased, but the wind howled with even greater fury. Shafts of moonlight funnelled through rents in the racing clouds, giving momentary glimpses of nightmare scenes of devastation. Gradually Mason became conscious of a deeper roar that welled from the south. It grew and grew, stilling even the thunder of the wind. The clouds above suddenly curled up like torn paper, the moonlight poured down, and they saw the pale vision of terror which accompanied the horrific sound. It was the sea, rushing in upon the tortured land!

CHAPTER EIGHTEEN

'To the fort!' Mason shouted, his voice a reedy whisper against the frightful detonation which seemed to rend the skies. 'To the fort! Maybe we can make it. If that catches us we're gone.'

With every ounce of strength they could muster, they raced for safety through water that covered their ankles, their knees. Mason whipped Sharon up and held her against his breast while he floundered on, Weed reeling and sloshing behind him. They were almost to the fort when the ground quivered to an impact greater than any before. The full force of the tidal wave had struck. As they scrambled up the steps to an open door, something huge and black flew past on the crest of a towering wave to land on the parade ground with a fearful crash.

'My God!' somebody yelled, 'it's a ship!'

It was—a three-masted schooner that had been swept shoreward from a hundred miles out in the Gulf and was thrown into the fort.

Nor was that the most weird thing which happened that night. A four-thousand-ton British steamer was torn from its moorings, carried over Pelican Spit and Pelican Island, and ultimately stranded on a thirty-foot bank in Chambers County, twenty-two miles from deep water!

In the tumult which followed, it seemed that the ponderous buildings of the fort would be uprooted and carried away like chips. The water rose four feet in as many seconds and washed completely over Galveston Island, leaving death and destruction in its wake.

'Will there be no end to it, Blaine?' Sharon asked as they sagged wearily against a wall that vibrated to the force of the wind.

'I think we've had the worst,' Mason replied. 'Soon the wind should begin to fall and there will be a period of calm. Then we'll catch it again, but I doubt if it will be as bad as before. We can only wait and see.'

Mason was right. That massive blow from the sea appeared to be the hurricane's master stroke. The wind gradually lessened in violence, became a gentle breeze, ceased altogether. Sharon pushed back her damp hair from her face.

'Come,' she said, 'there's still work to do.' Silently the two men followed her into the night.

The sky overhead was clear, blazing with stars, but circling the rim of the horizon were dark banks of cloud, purplish, ominous and threatening.

Leaving the fort, the three searched shattered houses for possible survivors, venturing into the deeper water as far as they dared, and found no living thing. Only death was abroad on the tossing waters.

A wall of blackness was mounting the northwest sky. Mason studied it and shook his head.

'Let's go back,' he said. 'We've done all we can, and the wind will be blowing again soon from the opposite direction.'

They returned to the fort and on a corner of the floor sank into the sodden sleep of utter exhaustion, while the hurricane roared away in search of new lands to lay waste.

The sun rose on indescribable scenes of horror. Some sections along the Gulf were entirely bare while others were covered with great hills of splintered timbers, twisted roofs and battered human bodies.

How many died that dreadful night? Nobody will ever know for sure. A conservative estimate placed the number at six thousand. Fifteen hundred acres of houses were totally destroyed. Eight thousand people were homeless, many of them destitute. Truly, tragedy walked naked through the land.

When Mason and his companions awakened, Sharon was so sore and stiff that Mason had to assist her to her feet. Weed tried to rise and sank back groaning.

A soldier came hurrying to them with coffee and a tray of food, of which they ate thankfully and in silence. Mason drained a final cup so hot he could hardly swallow it and said,

'You two stay here and rest. I'm going to the Hall, if it's still standing, and see what I can learn. I'll be back soon.'

On his way to the Hall, Mason paused in front of a building whose roof had collapsed. It was the Crystal Bar.

A group of men, including a police officer, had just carried two bodies out of the wreckage. One was long, lean, cadaverous. His unseeing, mismated eyes glared up at the sun drenched sky. On his lips was a toothy, sardonic grin. Long Tommy Hordle appeared to see something grotesquely humorous even in death.

The other body was big and bulky, and Sam Gulden's dead hand clutched a stout canvas sack.

'Wonder what's in it?' remarked the policeman. With some difficulty he loosened the grip of the stiffened fingers, upending the bag and dumped its contents, several sodden packets of bills of large denomination.

'Whe-ew!' he exclaimed, 'must be thirty-five or forty thousand dollars there!'

'If he hadn't stopped to tie on to that poke he might have got out alive,' observed one of the men. 'We found him right by the door.'

Mason's scalp prickled. He walked on, hurriedly.

At the Hall, order was slowly evolving from chaos. A relief committee was organized, with Blaine Mason to head it, and a department of safety which functioned until martial law could be established. All able-bodied survivors were impressed for the task of finding and caring for the injured and cleaning up the city.

Late that afternoon the Island Queen steamed into port under forced draft bearing the precious cargo of blankets, warm clothing, food and medicines provided by Blaine Mason's wise foresight.

'I don't know how the devil we got here without blowing up,' said Captain Peter Blake. 'The safety valves were tied down and the Lord only knows what the pressure in the boilers was. But we made it!'

For the next few days, Galveston had to indeed live up to its motto—I Alone! For Galveston was strictly on its own and had to be sufficient unto itself. Then aid came—money, supplies, the Red Cross, thirty thousand labourers supplied by the state, credit. The real work of rehabilitation began.

Against a recurrence of such a disaster, two vast engineering projects were proposed and plans laid for their undertaking. A mighty sea wall would be built, seven and a half miles long, fifteen feet wide at its base and five at its top, which would be seventeen feet above mean low tide. A twenty-seven-foot wide breakwater would be constructed of granite blocks. The level of the city would be raised as high as the sea wall on the Gulf side, sloping from there to the natural level of the bay. Zoning regulations would be adopted.

Soon, however, it became evident that the

city's problem could not be solved under its charter and form of government, or under the existing charter of any other American municipality. Conferences were held. Finally Blaine Mason rose with a proposal.

'Gentlemen,' he said, 'I have a suggestion, consisting only of a rough outline which, if it appears plausible, can be put into shape by wiser heads better versed in governmental affairs. I suggest that elected commissioners, say five in number, serve collectively as a legislative body and individually as administrators of the several departments. One commissioner, elected mayor or chosen by his colleagues, would function as president of the commission, each other commissioner being the head of an administrative department. Thus we'd eliminate the overlapping of authority with resulting conflict and the inevitable snarling of red tape that's plaguing us now. What do you think?'

The city leaders glanced at one another, nodded their heads. Honest John rose to his feet.

'Son,' he said, 'I believe you've hit on something. It'll take conferences and a lot of planning and thinking to iron out the rough spots and put it into effect, but I believe you've hit on something.'

Again there was a general nodding of agreement.

So was born the famous 'Galveston Plan,'

later to be called the Commission form of government, and to be adopted by hundreds of cities and towns in America and Europe.

Chauncey Weed, fully recovered and once more his jaunty self, hunted up Mason and Sharon.

'Well, it appears things are pretty well under control, and the trains are running again,' he said. 'So I'm on my way tomorrow to the Bradded L ranch and my belated wedding. I hope our best man and maid of honour can make it, too.'

'We will,' Mason promised smilingly. 'But I'm afraid you'll have to put up with a best man and a *matron* of honour. Sharon and I are headed for the courthouse right now. The judge will slip a double rig on us.'

Later, Mason paused outside the courthouse and gazed up at the words graven in the granite of the lofty pediment.

' "I Alone," ' he translated for Sharon's benefit. 'My motto.'

'It *was* your motto, but no more,' she replied softly. 'For now you are not alone!'

We hope you have enjoyed this Large Print book. Other Chivers Press or Thorndike Press Large Print books are available at your library or directly from the publishers.

For more information about current and forthcoming titles, please call or write, without obligation, to:

Chivers Large Print
published by BBC Audiobooks Ltd
St James House, The Square
Lower Bristol Road
Bath BA2 3BH
UK
email: bbcaudiobooks@bbc.co.uk
www.bbcaudiobooks.co.uk

OR

Thorndike Press
295 Kennedy Memorial Drive
Waterville
Maine 04901
USA
www.gale.com/thorndike
www.gale.com/wheeler

All our Large Print titles are designed for easy reading, and all our books are made to last.